AVENUE OF CHAMPIONS

CONOR KERR

AVENUE OF CHAMPIONS

NIGHTWOOD EDITIONS

2021

Nightwood Editions
P.O. Box 1779
Gibsons, BC VON 1VO
Canada
www.nightwoodeditions.com

COVER DESIGN: Carleton Wilson
TYPOGRAPHY: Carleton Wilson

Nightwood Editions acknowledges the support of the Canada Council for the Arts, the Government of Canada, and the Province of British Columbia through the BC Arts Council.

This book has been produced on 100% post-consumer recycled, ancient-forest-free paper, processed chlorine-free and printed with vegetable-based dyes.

Printed and bound in Canada.

LIBRARY AND ARCHIVES CANADA CATALOGUING IN PUBLICATION

Title: Avenue of champions / Conor Kerr.
Names: Kerr, Conor, author.
Identifiers: Canadiana (print) 2021024562X | Canadiana (ebook) 20210245646 | ISBN 9780889714182 (softcover) | ISBN 9780889714199 (HTML)
Subjects: LCGFT: Novels.
Classification: LCC PS8621.E7636 A95 2021 | DDC C813/.6—dc23

PROLOGUE:
THE LAST BIG DANCE

We ran out of hooch at that last big barn dance. It was good timing because the mounties showed up right afterwards and busted up the party. They came roaring in with their usual big fuss and grandeur, pretending they were real tough guys and not just a bunch of hooligans looking for booze and drunk ladies. Granny hated when they showed up. She didn't want anyone in a uniform drinking the hooch she made and she didn't want anyone interrupting her fiddle music, least of all the mounties. Granny hated them. She has her reasons. They're always showing up at her place looking for the stills, taking all the canned meat and vegetables from the cold cellar, busting up the horses and lighting the wood pile on fire. They tried to bust her up once too but she smacked the man's chubby cheeks red with her spoon and threatened to let loose her wolves on them. She didn't have any wolves, but the city boys from Ontario who were posted on their first tour to northern Alberta didn't know that. So instead of busting up Granny, they settled for busting up the barn dances.

That same night, Uncle Jim went through the ice on the Amisk River on our ride back home. He was right pickled and somehow managed to fall out of the back of the wagon, off the bridge and went all the way up to his neck in the muck and water even though the river's only about three feet deep in that spot and he's six foot plus. He kept screaming bloody murder about the beavers dragging him under the ice. Said he'd be back to "light them toothy fuckers up." My cousins and I threw him the rope, tied it off to the wagon. Granny got the horses going and we pulled him right out of his hole and over the ice to the bank. We got him out of his clothes and wrapped in a woollen blanket in the back of the straw-laden wagon. First thing he did was grab a bottle of hooch he must have stashed in the straw and took a big swig. Then he winked at me.

"You and me girl, it's just you and me," he said with a moonshine slur before he passed out. My cousins and I killed time on the rest of the ride home by putting straw up his nose. We tried to see how many pieces we could get up there before he would swat them out in his drunken stupor.

"Jim never could handle his hooch," Granny said as we unhitched the horses and headed into her cabin.

I moved into Granny's one-room shack shortly after my tenth birthday in 1942. Granny had just celebrated her birthday by shooting a two-year-old bull moose off her front porch right between the eyes with her old lever action rifle. All the family and neighbours came over to help butcher up the moose and celebrate Granny's good aim. It was at that party that my parents told me I wasn't coming back with them. My mother and father had just had their ninth child and there was no room in their own one-bedroom cabin. It didn't bother me none. I liked the idea of having my own bed and not sharing it with four of my brothers and sisters. Uncle Jim had recently left Granny's to go and fight the Nazis over in Europe.

My parents told me that Granny was going to need a hand around her cabin. I figured that meant chopping wood, getting water and shooting the odd deer or bird, tasks I was well suited to, having done them for as long as I could remember. In reality it meant spending days doing all those tasks plus carrying the fifty-pound sacks of grain half a mile back into the woods to the old copper still. The trail to the still wasn't defined like the one that led back to my parents' house. It was rough, tough walking. You were continually dodging around the fallen birch and pine trees and old spruce boughs with all that grain or wheat or corn or barley or horse feed on your shoulders. Worst of it was covering your tracks on the way out. If even a little hint of a trail was showing, a footprint in the snow, a tree moved out of the way, even leaves crunched up, Granny would hammer on you with her wooden spoon.

"You going to lead dem mounties right to it," she'd yell. "Can't cover a track, walking around out there like a goddamn moniyaw."

At night, we'd sit around the wood-burning stove drinking spruce needle tea from the cast iron pot permanently steeping on top of the stove. My night tasks were to make sure that pot was permanently full of water by melting snow in it and adding cups of spruce needles Granny had dried out during the summer. My other task was to place the beads on or thread Granny's beading needle. In the last few years, her hands had taken to shaking and she couldn't do either anymore. But once I got those on there for her, she'd be flying through the tanned moose hide creating elaborate floral designs. While she beaded, she'd tell stories of the land and all our relations that lived here with us. She told me about where mosquitoes come from, and why you should never trust a government official, a banker or a mountie. She talked about long lean months in the winter when her, my mother and Uncle Jim wouldn't have anything to eat except for the donations from some of the neighbour families who were also on the verge of starving. How she would have to do the hunting since there wasn't a man around to go and get deer, birds and moose. She talked about Jim, and how good of a shot he was with the rifle, how he learned to shoot animals in the head to ease their suffering and preserve more of the meat, how he had been doing that since he was six years old. Then she'd laugh and talk about how she pitied those Germans who got in the way of Jim's rifle.

Sometimes one of Granny's regular customers, usually one of the town folks from St. Lina or St. Paul, would make a special request for a fancy bottle. They'd show up with husked corn instead of the usual grain. Granny liked making corn moonshine. With the low-end stuff, she would never bother checking it or caring what kind of proof it was. She would just bottle it up and send it off. With the corn mash moonshine, she would take extra time. She'd wait until the dog's head got going, about a week after the mash first got cooking, watching for the large single bubbles coming up every twenty to thirty seconds. She'd slop it back, pouring it onto itself to kick out the cap from the still. Then she'd wait another three days until she really got shining. When she figured it was done, she'd fill half a jar from the still, take it in her right hand and hit the wrinkled palm of her left hand with the jar three times. Not four times, not two times, but three times. She'd turn the jar on its side and the shine would separate into three consistent pools if it had been done right.

"Hundo-three proof, looking good." She'd take a little sip. She never drank the shine, would just sip a tablespoon's worth to check the flavouring. "She's good, my girl. Let's get this bottled up and out of here."

Granny and her husband were both little kids when the Canadian government dissolved the Papaschase First Nation. All the Band members had been off hunting or at the Fort and the mounties and the Indian agent took advantage of that and declared the First Nation null and void. When her family tried to go back to their shacks to get some supplies, the mounties were already there and everything was up in flames. Granny fled with her family to the bush north of St. Lina, Alberta. She lived there, married a man from the Papaschase whose family also fled to the bush. The two of them started having kids, but then Granny's husband up and died one day. My mother told me he died from heartbreak from being forced off the land he had loved. Uncle Jim told me it was TB. Either way, Granny never talked about her husband. And she never talked about the Papaschase land she had grown up on. But she loved woodpeckers. Anytime a woodpecker would be hanging around the cabin she would spend all

11

day rolling handmade cigarettes, drinking tea and watching the bird work its way around a white poplar tree.

Uncle Jim showed up back at Granny's cabin a few days after I turned fifteen. He had spent a year after the war "showing those Québécois ladies how to really jig." Then he had run out of money and hopped a train back out to Alberta. When he first arrived, we'd sit around Granny's cabin night after night and listen to him tell stories about Europe and the war. Everyone who was anyone plus a few others from the area would be over at Granny's drinking 'shine and listening to Jim describe how the underwear looked on this lady from Trois-Rivières.

"You watch out, she might be your cousin," Granny would yell, smiling with a cigarette hanging out of her mouth as she ladled out drinks for the listeners. That summer was a real party. We went through more 'shine than we had in a long time, partly because of the nightly story session, partly because Jim drank it all day every day.

Even if Uncle Jim drank the still dry the night before, he would be up for the sunrise. Didn't matter if the sun was coming up at 8:30 in the winter or 4:30 in the summer, he would rise with it. I woke up every morning to the *thwock* of the axe splitting birch from the wood pile. The smell of tobacco trailed behind him as he walked past my bed carrying an armful of wood for the stove. I always tried to wait until the stove had the cabin roasting before I got out from underneath the wool blanket.

The morning after Jim fell through the ice on the Amisk River he was moving like a bear with an itch. After the stove got fired up, I could sense him standing right above me, but I refused to open my eyes, hoping he would get bored and wander off to check on the stills. He poked me in the gut with the barrel of the 30-30 lever action rifle we kept by the door.

"Hey girl, those beavers are probably dragging some kid under the ice right now." He poked me again with the barrel of the gun. "Might even be one of your brothers or sisters."

"Get out of here, you reek like booze you old bum." I turned over and pulled the woollen blanket over my head. "That thing better not be loaded."

"How would you feel about that?" Jim said.

"Don't really care."

He wasn't going to leave me alone. The stove had taken the frost out of the air in the cabin. Jim sat on the chair across from my bed and started rolling a cigarette.

"Roll me one of those and I'll help you out," I said.

Jim finished rolling a smoke and passed it to me. Then he started rolling another one for himself.

"I found the spot. Ain't no more beavers going to be dragging poor unsuspecting folk under the water any longer."

We saddled up the wagon horses. They both snorted and stomped their appreciation for going for just a little ride and not hauling the wagon around. Granny walked by us on her way down to the still. She nodded at us, the customary cigarette hanging out of her lips unlit until she finished her walk. Granny never smoked while walking.

"If you see a moose, take that instead of the beavers. We could use the meat," she said.

Jim gave a faux salute and we set off through the bush. It was a good dozen miles or so to the spot on the river where Jim had gone through the ice. I settled into the saddle and lit the cigarette Jim had rolled for me. The sun had a warmth to it that we hadn't felt in months. All around us the land was waking up from its winter rest. Birds chirped and fought between the bare branches of the poplar and birch trees, squirrels chattered to announce our arrival as we passed underneath them on the trail, a couple coyotes howled in the distance. The worst of winter was behind us and everything in the bush was out in full celebration. Even Jim seemed to momentarily forget that he had a score to settle with some beavers.

The melting snow had left a series of cracks through the ice on the Amisk River, and you could clearly see the spot where Jim had fallen through after the party. There was a thin layer of ice over the hole and in the busted-up area where he had been dragged out. Whisky jacks swooped all around us checking out what we were doing in their area, their grey and black feathers bristling with the prospect of a free meal.

"awas," Jim yelled at them, then muttered, "You're giving away our goddamn position. Damn beavers will know we're coming now."

"I think the yelling gave us away, not the whisky jacks," I said.

"No one cares what you think," Jim grumbled and pulled a jar of hooch out of his saddlebag. "Shouldn't be too shooken yah think?" He took a big swig.

"Not many beavers around here," I said.

"Oh they're coming, believe me, those toothy motherfuckers are coming."

Jim and I hopped down from our horses and tethered them to a couple birch trees. They immediately started pawing up the snow to get at the old grass underneath it. The horses both seemed more than content to bask in the sun and eat the grass while we figured out the best place to watch for beavers. Jim made sure to bring the hooch, rifle and the rolling tobacco from his bag while I kicked snow out of the way to try and make a dry spot for us to sit. For the next couple hours, Jim and I sat beside the creek and he drank the first bottle of hooch, and then the second bottle of hooch, and then started to get into a third. At some point during the second bottle Jim started firing the 30-30 randomly at the ice.

"Think I got one there."

"Think the bullet ricocheted off the ice, Uncle."

"Yeah, ricocheted right into a beaver. Just like I was planning." He fired another one. "See got another one."

"Don't know if you did, Uncle."

"How many men you ever shot kid? Huh? I think I know when I hit a beaver or not." Jim's dark brown eyes were rolling circles in his head. "Think that's enough killing for today. Let's head back and see what Granny's doing," he slurred.

I got the horses and saddled them up while Jim kept watch for beavers and rolled smokes for the ride back. As soon as I helped Jim up on his horse, he lit one of the smokes and then immediately fell asleep. I grabbed the reins from his mare and hitched her up to my horse and we went down the trail. The animal noise and chatter had faded with the setting sun. The only sound now was the snorts and snores from Jim as he half dozed and half smoked from behind me on the trail. At one point he woke up from his drunk, looked at me and said, "You know any Cree?"

"Not much," I answered. "How about you?"

He had already fallen asleep before I finished asking. The smell of hooch on him was so strong it overpowered the mare's breath, which wasn't exactly mint fresh. All I could think of was getting him dropped off in a bed back at Granny's.

As we got closer to Granny's cabin, I noticed something was happening. I could hear shouts coming from inside. I stopped the horses, hopped down, and snuck up to the cabin. The shouts kept getting louder. It sounded like a couple of rough male voices with Granny's mixed in. As I got closer, I realized I should have grabbed the 30-30 from Jim. Then I decided that it might be some of the family from down the road getting into it after a few too many drinks. I eased up a bit with this thought and walked through the woods with a bold step. I was almost at the cabin when Granny came flying out the door, and not of her own free will. Two mounties followed, both their pale cheeks red with rage. I ducked behind the wood pile and watched as the one hit Granny across the face, knocking her back down.

"Damn squaw, you're going to tell us where the still is or we're going to burn this all to the ground," the one who hit Granny yelled. The other mountie went and kicked her while she was on the ground.

I panicked. Granny swore at them in Cree and got up. The mounties kept pushing her back down. I gotta get Jim, I decided, forgetting that he was wasted off his tree. The mounties, too obsessed with Granny, didn't notice me start running back toward where I had left the horses and Jim. The shouting followed me. When I got there, I found the horses, but no Jim. *Stupid drunk, probably passed out under a tree nearby,* I thought. I had to figure out what to do about Granny. I thought of riding to my parents' cabin and getting my father. It was only about fifteen to twenty minutes at a full gallop. In the distance the screaming continued. I was about to hop up on the horse when I heard the gunshot. And then another gunshot. And then another.

Back at Granny's cabin, I found Jim standing over the bodies of the two mounties pointing his 30-30 rifle at them, red blood splattered across the white snow. One had been shot in the arm and the leg, the other just in the arm. Their firearms had been thrown into a pile over by the cabin's steps. They stared at Jim with horror. Both young men from somewhere in Ontario, never guessing that they would be facing death in the northern Alberta bush. Jim held the rifle with the authority of someone who had killed before.

"Well now, why would you two go and beat up on an old lady for something as silly as moonshine?" Jim asked, his voice calm now, lacking the drunken stupor of earlier. Both the mounties stared at him, neither daring to answer. The one who had been shot twice started hyperventilating. "Alright, go on both of you back inside the cabin. We gotta get you bandaged up." Jim prodded them with his rifle. Neither of them could move on account of having been shot up, so I took to dragging them inside on the sled we normally used for wood. They were both heavy boys, definitely had been eating well inside the depot back in St. Paul, and there was a good yellow piss stain on the snow mixed in with the blood under where the one guy had been laying. Inside Granny's cabin she had been prepping bandages and tourniquets and got to fixing up their bleeding. She wrapped them both in woollen blankets and sat them down by the wood stove to help with the shock.

"Relax, no one's going to die tonight," Jim said. "But if either of you ever think of coming back to this area, well, that's going to be a different story." He lit a cigarette from where he sat in the chair with the 30-30 pointing at them. Granny finished fixing the mounties up and started pouring tea. I stood back in the corner trying to stay close to the door or a window in case Jim changed his mind.

"After we finish this tea, thank you Granny, by the way, you two boys are going to head back into town and tell the sergeant that you got in a fight with a couple of beavers out by the Amisk River. Got it?" Both the mounties nodded their heads as fast as they could. "Or as we said in Quebec, a good old castor fight." Jim exhaled smoke in their faces. "Now you going to thank Granny for being so kind as to make you tea?"

"Th-th-th-thanks," they both said.

"Now let's get you boys on those horses."

As the mounties set off on the horses toward St. Paul, Granny, Jim and I turned back to where the 30-30 cartridges sat in the snow surrounded by blood and piss stains.

"I think it's about time you headed back to your parents' for a bit," Granny said to me. "At least until your goddamn trigger-happy uncle figures out his place."

"They would have shot all three of us if I hadn't stepped in," Jim said. "Should've known they would have been waiting until after we took off. Goddamn beavers."

"Mounties, Jim, mounties," Granny said. Her eyes were fixed on the blood. "Hooch is getting to that brain of yours."

"You know what, I think I'm going to go and fix those beavers up right now," Jim said. Without turning back to face us he walked over to where his horse was still standing saddled up from earlier that night. He hopped on the horse and headed back down the trail we had come from. The darkness of the night quickly enveloped him.

"Should I go after him?" I asked Granny.

"Leave him be. Come on, let's get this cleaned up."

Jim didn't come back that night. Granny told me not to worry about him and to save my own skin and head back down to my parents'. She figured the mounties would be coming back with everything they had. The next day, instead of heading in that direction, I went toward the river where I found Jim's horse tied up to the same birch tree that he and I had tethered up to the day before. A couple of empty hooch jars lay haphazardly in the snow beside a dozen cigarette butts that led in a trail toward a hole in the ice that hadn't quite frozen over yet.

1. BRIDGES

"Let's get the fuck out of here, Daniel." Jason steamrolled his five-foot-five scrawny frame into the room we shared at the group home. He had a black eye and paper towel shoved up his nose to stop the bleeding. "Guy thinks he's so tough, I'll show him." Jason started shoving clothes into a torn-up black back-pack. I had been busy thinking about this girl from school. We'd been playing grounders at lunch and I loved the way her dark curly hair bounced when she jumped from the slide all the way over to the monkey bars. I had this dream that she was into me too and we could be a couple, hold hands, maybe even make out. Jason's bloody nose barged right into that fantasy. I hopped down from the top bunk, grabbed my bag and stuffed in my other pair of jeans, a couple pairs of ratty boxers, shirts and an Oilers hoodie. All my worldly possessions packed up in fifteen seconds.

"Eddy?" I asked. Jason just nodded. I'd been there too. Eddy liked to drink his way through the Valleyview Pub and then beat up on us when he got back to the group home. First kid he stumbled across got it. His wife just sat there smoking and ignoring, waiting for the next cheque from the government to come in to fuel her smokes and pills and Eddy's booze. I knew from my last foster home that that money was supposed to go toward us and I made the mistake once of asking if I could take guitar lessons. Eddy answered that with his right fist.

We walked out of the room and into the common area we shared with a couple other kids. One little guy was playing *Mario Kart* on the N64. Jason went over, grabbed the controller out of his hand, unplugged the machine and put it in his back-pack. The kid was about to say something, then Jason moved like he was going to punch the kid and he decided against it.

"We can pawn this," Jason said to me as we left the house. We knew from previous experience that Eddy and his wife would wait a couple days before calling the cops. They'd let Jason's injuries heal a bit so they could pass it off as a couple teenagers getting in fights with each other if the cops asked any questions. They never did ask. The last time we ran we didn't make it far. Jason figured we'd take the shortest route over the bridge into downtown. Only problem was we didn't take the sidewalk, just the road, and ended up in the middle of a bridge with cars ripping past us and no place to go. Someone must have called it in and the cops picked us up and dropped us back off at the group home. The time before that though we were gone for a couple days. We holed up in this old cave underneath the patio of the Fairmont Macdonald Hotel. It was a beautiful spot, the kind that every kid dreams of for a fort, and a total coincidence that we stumbled across it when we were lost in the bushes searching for the stairs to head up from the river valley toward downtown. We could hear the slurps, smacks and laughter from the people eating over our heads. All of them clueless that a couple kids had spent the last few nights eating stolen cans of Alphagetti and bags of chips underneath them.

This time we headed straight for Whyte Avenue. Jason had a cousin that hung around the Mill Creek Bridge and the youth shelter there. T.J. scared me, guy always had a bunch of homeless dudes and ladies hanging around, or other tougher kids. I wasn't that bothered by them though. The thing that scared me the most was his eyes. They were black pits that looked through you. Jason had similar eyes but his seemed to turn on and off. T.J.'s were always black and they bore right through you. First time I met him he pulled a butterfly knife out of his back pocket and started spinning it around, then held it up to my throat. "You ever been in a knife fight?" he asked me. I just shook my head and tried not to piss myself. He moved the knife away then pulled his shirt off and started showing me all these scars he claimed were stab wounds. "Guys always trying to get me but I'm hard as fuck," T.J. said. "And the babes love it you know." I didn't have any knife scars, didn't really want one either.

We found T.J. under the Mill Creek Bridge. He was sitting with two girls who both looked younger than Jason and me. All three of them were wearing oversized black hoodies that read *Cocaine & Caviar* on them. I wondered if the girl from my English class would ever hang out underneath a bridge that always smelled like backed-up sewer and urinal cakes. She was probably off reading or doing homework, playing with her family—I wasn't quite sure what happened in nice family homes. I just imagine there are lots of chips and pop and other food there. We dodged around the broken bottle and light bulb glass and needles to get to where T.J. and the girls were sitting on a concrete slab. Overhead you could hear the continuous drone of traffic as vehicles moved across the bridge. The bigger trucks would rattle the foundation a bit, the semis and fire trucks would make it feel like the slabs were going to pick up and buck you off.

"Sup cuz?" T.J. asked when he saw it was Jason.

"You know, looking for a smoke, you got any?" Jason asked.

"Got a buck? Shit ain't free," T.J. replied. Jason didn't say anything. T.J. tossed him a smoke from a pack of Canadian Classics. "Guy's gotta take care of his fam."

"You got a lighter?" Jason asked.

"What, you want me to smoke the damn thing for you too? Pathetic, bud."

"Hey can I have a smoke too?" One of the girls sat up. I thought I recognized her from a Boys and Girls Club camp last summer. I tried to catch her eye to see if she recognized me but she wouldn't look anywhere near me. T.J. tossed her a smoke, she lit it and passed it to the other girl.

"Fuck, am I the only one that works around here?" T.J. said. He started laughing and then stopped abruptly when he noticed me.

"You brought your little butt buddy," he said to Jason. "Guy's not a narc is he?"

"Hell no, I wouldn't hang out with no narcs," Jason replied. I stayed silent. I didn't want another knife to my throat. "Check out what we got." Jason reached into his backpack and pulled out the N64. "Stole it from the group home."

"Shit man, you gotta be careful, cops will throw you in juvie right quick if they find you with stolen goods my dude. Better let me take care of it," T.J. said.

Bad idea, I thought. *You give that to him and we're never seeing it again.* I looked over at Jason and saw that he had a similar thought from the expression on his face. Jason also thought T.J. was the toughest shit around and talked about him all the time.

"Yeah I know. That's why we're gonna go pawn it right now," Jason replied.

"Let's roll then. I know this great pawn shop just down the Avenue. Guy gives me a real good price." T.J. hopped down from the ledge and the two girls followed.

The five of us took off walking down Whyte Avenue. T.J. and Jason led, I followed right behind them and the two girls trailed me. We all had our backpacks on, loaded up with whatever we owned. Every person we walked by did their best to ignore our existence. I don't think anyone else I was with noticed, but I definitely did. The obvious way they tried to avoid our presence. But shit, I was part of something, we were going to go get cash for the N64. I had no idea what we were going to do after that but all that mattered was that we would get this cash, get rid of that thing and then carry on.

After you turn twelve the foster families don't want you. You go from cute little kid to teenage criminal in a year. First time you do anything even remotely wrong you're out. I had lived with these foster parents for a few years. Then one day I lost track of time playing grounders at the park with some other neighbourhood kids. When I got home, my bags were packed and the social worker was waiting. She took me to Eddy and his wife's group home. I ran into my foster parents again at this Children's Services Christmas feast thing that same year. They had another little kid with them and did their best to avoid looking at me. I had really liked living with them too. They let me take guitar lessons and play sports. We ate the same food for dinner. There was none of that macaroni and hot dogs for the foster kids while the real family ate chicken thing happening. They really cared about me, you could tell. At least they did until I got too old. Jason showed up at the group home not long after I was there. Our fathers were apparently from the same Métis community, not that either of us had ever met them. But the social workers figured that putting us together would help with our identity or some shit like that.

There were a couple old street boys set up in the unused doorway of this shady liquor store. The one guy was wrapped in multiple tattered blankets even though it was a beautiful warm day outside. He was shivering away and his face was covered in pockmarks and scars. The other guy was sitting beside him wearing greasy sweatpants covered in numerous brown stains that could have been anything from shit to blood to mud. The sweatpants man had forty or so cigarette butts laid out on the ground and he was scraping the leftover tobacco out of each one of them. T.J. stopped to talk to them. Jason stayed with him. I walked up to this bench a bit down the block and sat down and the two girls followed me. They sat down beside me. We were in front of a rundown strip mall that had an old convenience store that mainly sold bongs, a liquor store and a karaoke VLT bar that had seen better days. Even though it was the middle of the afternoon about ten people were hanging around outside the bar smoking and taking pulls from a plastic mickey.

"I'm Daniel," I said to the girls, trying to make my voice sound deeper than it was. They both stared at me and then started whispering to each other. I pulled my hoodie up over my head and leaned forward. "Did I see you at the Boys and Girls camp last year?" I asked the one girl. Her eyes got a bit wider but she just shook her head.

"She would never go to one of those dorky-ass camps," her friend answered for her.

T.J. and Jason caught up to us on the bench. Jason had bummed a smoke off some guy walking past and lit it. He was waving it around and blowing smoke that hung over us in the stale summer air.

"Okay, we're good. Buddy up there said he'd boot for us when we get the money," T.J. said. "I think we'll get a lot of cash for this bad boy. Now if one of you dipshits was smart enough to grab more games…"

"You should have grabbed the games Daniel, the fuck you thinking?" Jason said. That was another reason I didn't really like being around T.J. Jason started to act more and more like him to try and impress everyone. I could see the N64 cords hanging out of a hole in T.J.'s backpack. At some point when they were talking Jason must have passed it over to him.

"I'm going to head down to the pawn shop. Guy wouldn't even think of buying from little kids like you all but he doesn't mind me," T.J. said. "Let's meet up at the stoner gazebo by the library in an hour."

"Think he's coming back?" I asked Jason.

"He fucking better, man. Guy's got my money," he replied. T.J. was due an hour ago. It was just the two of us. We'd lost the girls when we walked by another group of people hanging around outside the old armoury youth shelter. We were now sitting in the gazebo watching the suburb tourists walk around the square checking out the art booths set up everywhere. They walked with the weightlessness of people who had never known how it felt to wake up alone every day. A light air to their steps and the buzz of laughter surrounding the din of their conversations. I hoped that T.J. wouldn't show up. I could care less about buying a bunch of booze or whatever their plan was. I didn't like the constant threat of violence that T.J. brought with him or the people who tended to latch on to that.

"Youth shelter closes their doors at ten. And we can't be drunk if we want to sleep there," I said.

"Who wants to sleep in that shithole with those street bums?" Jason replied. "Besides it's gorgeous out tonight. Worst comes to worst we'll crash at T.J.'s. He's got a sick apartment he told me. Big flat-screen TV and tons of weed and beers."

"Why aren't we there right now?" I asked.

"You think shit's free man? We gotta pitch in you know," Jason replied. I was still trying to get my head around how I could possibly pitch in. Everything I owned was on my back and no one wanted those ratty-ass clothes.

A group of older guys and girls, maybe university students, walked by smoking and drinking beer.

"Hey can I bum a smoke?" Jason asked them.

"Get out of here kid. How old are you even?" One of the guys responded. Jason's eyes glazed over and he stood up and started walking toward the group. I stood up, pulled my hood over my head and followed. I knew how to pitch in on this at least.

"Fuck you say to me?" Jason asked.

"Chill out kid," the guy said over his shoulder as the group kept walking away from us. We followed right behind. I saw Jason put his hand in his pocket and knew that he was clenching his fingers around a lighter. He pulled his hand out and kept his fist balled up around it.

"Call me a kid again."

"Kid, seriously get out of here." The guy turned around to stand up to him. Jason smashed him in the nose with his right fist then dragged the metal from the lighter back across his cheek slicing into the skin. The guy dropped and blood started running out of the cut. We turned and ran, carried by the screams of the group. Back into the crowd milling about the square. The people who always looked right through us.

"Head wounds always look worse than they are," I said to Jason. "I'm sure the guy's fine."

"He asked for it. Why did he ask for it? I didn't want to do that." Jason and I were sitting behind the same A&W that T.J. had disappeared behind a few hours before. We were on the other side of the tracks. The suburb crowds never went over to this side of the tracks, unless they were on a poverty sightseeing expedition or looking for cheap greasy burgers. "Think he called the cops?" Jason asked. He was sitting on an old picnic table shaking a green Nabob coffee can filled with smoke butts.

"Nah, no way. No one calls the cops," I said.

"Rich people call the cops."

"You ever know anyone who called the cops?" I asked.

"I've never known anyone who was rich," Jason replied.

Jason asked me once if I had ever met my family. We were laying on the bunk beds back at the group home. There was no rail on the top bunk where I slept and I was always scared that some night I was going to roll right off and fall down to the floor. I would usually throw my pillows down hoping that they might brace my fall if it ever came. I would lay there awake for hours on end watching this old red lava lamp that some past kid had left in the room. It had this cycle where the blobs would shoot rapidly to the top and then stay there for a bit before slowly falling down and then shooting up in big round blobs for the rest of the night. I watched it go through this over and over again. When Jason wanted to talk, he would start subtly kicking my mattress above him. If I didn't respond the kicks would start getting more and more forceful until finally I acknowledged him.

I told him that my granny and grandpa come to visit once in a while. They showed up at my old foster home with the social worker and took me out for supper at Boston Pizza once. That was the first time I had been to a Boston Pizza and Granny told me to order anything. We ended up splitting a large Hawaiian pizza and some wings and I'm pretty sure I drank my weight in root beer. When they dropped me off later that night they said they'd be back to visit soon. That they were working on getting permission for Charlie and I to come and live with them.

"I think I see my father sometimes," Jason told me. "He's downtown in the Métis housing projects east of Boyle Street. I think I saw him at the downtown library once and then another time when I was on the bus to school. He's a big tough guy. Bushy brown beard, balding a bit, but he looks like he can beat up anyone he wants to. He had this sweet black leather jacket on with a bunch of patches, probably in a gang, you know."

This was the one and only time we talked about our families. It wasn't cool to bring up family in the group home. I didn't tell Jason about my older brother Charlie, who was in another group home, or supposed to be at least. Most of us had a similar story and no one wanted to hear it. There was always that one kid who would never shut up about how someone was coming to get him. How he wouldn't be there the next day. The kind of kid who always had his bag ready to go. No one liked that kid. And his family would never come. I didn't want to be that kid. So even though Granny said she was coming to get me, I wasn't going to bank on it.

"Where do you think we can find T.J. at?" I asked. Not that it was something I was entirely interested in, but Jason was still sulking around as if he had been the one who got punched.

"Who knows. Probably that stupid bridge," Jason replied. Then he mumbled something about his money.

"Should we head that way?" I asked. It was getting closer to ten p.m. and I had every intention of making sure I was in the doors of that youth shelter before they locked up for the night.

T.J. was back where we found him earlier that day, sitting under the bridge. This time the two girls had been replaced by the two guys who'd been lounging outside the liquor store earlier. Besides the location, you could never tell that anything about them had changed. One guy was still wrapped in his blankets lying out on the concrete slab under the bridge. The other guy was sitting with his legs hanging over the slab about a foot off the ground, rolling cigarettes from a baggie of street ash. The summer sun still lit up the areas around the bridge but underneath it only the hollow black of T.J.'s eyes shone through the inevitable creeping darkness of night. He was pacing back and forth in front of the two guys. He would walk ten paces and then turn on a dime and walk another ten paces. All you could hear was him sucking the mucus back up his nose in a loud *shronk*. He didn't notice us until we were almost beside him.

"Holy shit, Jason man. Jason my boy," T.J. said. He ran up to Jason and put him in a headlock. "Just the cousin I wanted to see," he continued.

"You get the cash?" Jason asked. He tried out his best tough guy voice but you could still hear the tremor in it.

"I got something even better than the cash. Something that you're going to love, my man."

"Whisky?" Jason asked.

"Even better, my man, even better." T.J. started pacing again, then abruptly stopped and looked at me. "Fuck's this?" he asked. "Cheeseburger want to get high too?"

I did not want to get high. I did not like being called Cheeseburger either, but T.J. had moved right up and in on my face. I could smell something rotten on his breath. Some sort of artificial stench. But I couldn't place it. His eyes locked with mine and I saw that chemical void of unpredictability. He kept sniffling and each sniffle seemed to echo warning signs through my head. I wanted to get the hell out of there more than anything.

"I would love to see that shit," he said. "Little dork all sped up ripping shit."

Jason laughed at that. Then he slung his backpack up onto the concrete slab. He hopped up after it. The guy rolling the cigarettes passed him one and he lit it up with that same lighter.

"So can I get some or what?" Jason asked.

"Gonna cost you," T.J. replied.

"I gave you that N64 earlier you were going to pawn," Jason said. "What happened to my cash from that?"

"Oh right. Yeah shit I forgot about that," T.J. said. He hopped up beside Jason. "You can smoke after he smokes." He pointed with his lips toward me.

"Fucking rights," Jason said. *Fuck that*, I thought. T.J. pulled a glass pipe out of his pocket and a tiny white baggie filled with the distinct shattered crystals of meth. He pulled out a crystal, placed it in the pipe and then passed it to me with a butane lighter.

"Smoke up, Cheeseburger," T.J. said. Jason's, the cigarette guy's, blanket man's, T.J.'s, all eyes were fixed on me. I'd smoked enough weed over the years to know the form. Pipe up, lighter out. My fingers searched for the choke. Maybe I could fake the inhale, just take it in and blow it back out, no lung action.

"The fuck you doing man? You gotta heat that shit up. Light up the bottom man." T.J. motioned to show where to hold the lighter underneath. Then he mimicked the flame on the glass. "Don't be pulling that junior high shit in here."

I thought of my Granny and what she would think if she saw where I was right now. I thought of the girl from school with the bouncy dark curls. I thought of Charlie who I hadn't seen in a long time.

"Time's up," T.J. said. I looked up in time for him to grab the pipe out of my hand and then punch me in the nose. Stars and those fuzzy TV dots blurred my eyes out and I fell over backwards. I could feel the warm flow of blood starting to drip out of my nose. I rolled over onto my side hoping that I didn't land on a needle. My vision cleared and I looked up at Jason. I was hoping that he would defend me. He didn't return the gaze. He was transfixed on the pipe that T.J. had just passed him. The flame was going and smoke started filling up the glass enclosure. Then they were both gone for a brief second until Jason exhaled what was left back into the under-bridge darkness.

"Hell yeah," he said. Then he leaned back. I watched as T.J. grabbed the pipe from him and put another piece of crystal in it.

I stood up and ran. Blood poured down from my nose and into my mouth. I tried to suck it back in, to drink it up, to let the flowing blood get me out from under that bridge.

"Run, Cheeseburger, run," I heard T.J. call after me, though it may have even been Jason. They weren't going to follow.

I kept running down the Avenue until I got to the doors of the youth shelter. A group of kids were still hanging outside smoking. That meant it was still open. I opened the door and headed over to where the social worker was checking people in. I tried to say something but the words weren't coming out.

I was still huffing from the sprint there. The social worker said something that I couldn't make out. The lights started spinning above me. And the floor felt so good. So clean and cool on my head as I laid down and closed my eyes.

I woke up in the emergency room. Eddy from the group home, a cop and my social worker were sitting there beside the bed. They asked me questions I couldn't answer. Who hit me? Where was Jason? Why did I leave? Did anything else hurt? Was I on drugs or alcohol? I closed my eyes and ignored them. As soon as I got back to the group home there would be another fist flying for my head. I tried to drown out their questions with thoughts of chips and pop and black bouncing curls in a game of grounders. I thought of my granny and a place to go home to.

2. SKATING CIRCLES

"We believe in the Avenue of Champions," the mayor announces to a small crowd standing in the outdoor rink. Most of the people in the crowd I've never seen before. They're all wearing suits and big black overcoats or are really done up in black pencil skirts, definitely no one from the neighbourhood. They look out of place next to the broken boards, chain-link fences and the graffiti that covers everything around the old outdoor community rink. Behind them, sitting around in the shadows are a bunch of local people from the neighbourhood. They're checking out what's happening. CBC, Global and CityNews are all here. They're jostling for position with the cameras, filming the mayor as he makes the announcement that they're putting money into revitalization of the rink. That's the new big word. *Revitalization.* You hear it all over the high school these days. That and the *We believe in the Avenue of Champions* slogan. They printed that one on big banners and hung them all around the decrepit rink.

"Bullshit," Charlie spits out a plug of chew.

In the background another speaker goes on stage and starts chanting, "We believe in the Avenue of Champions." The crowd doesn't join in. He's echoed only by the other people in fancy black clothes. That makes me smile a bit.

"Only thing those fucks believe in is money."

"Man, if they build us a new rink I don't care what they fucking believe in," one of Charlie's buddies replies.

I don't expect to see any of those politicians around the outdoor community rink after this. This is just their sightseeing tour. Once the speeches are over, the people from the neighbourhood come to check it out. They hate the thought that they'll end up in one of the camera shots or an interview. Granny's friends love nothing more than making fun of one of their friends they see on the news. I wouldn't mind getting interviewed. Just to see what it's like. I have some good stories too. I could tell them about how this Jason kid torched the skate shack. I'd let them think it was some crazy-ass pyro strolling for burns. Then I'd let them in on the secret that he just fell asleep with a dart in his mouth and it was too close to the plastic water bottle filled with gas that he had been huffing. I wouldn't say his name, of course, but I'd let them know that these things don't just burn down. Those of us who grew up here, we don't need to believe in the Avenue of Champions. We know it already.

The city's gonna put up new boards to replace the rotting ones that a good slapshot, hell even the flick of a puck can blast right through, sending splinters everywhere. They'll replace the broken chicken wire around the back ends of the rink and actually give us a couple good nets and put new heaters in the skate shack. Hell, they're even going to build a new skate shack. They announce all of this today and then we're going to have the annual cops-versus-neighbourhood hockey game. At the beginning of the winter one of the sporting goods stores in Edmonton dumps off a load of used gear for the neighbourhood, and there's always a big scramble to get in and grab a good pair of skates or gloves or shoulder pads. Lots of the sticks are used ones from the Oilers and people go crazy thinking they have McDavid's or Lucic's old twig. They think they'll get the same hands or dangles or something. Most families end up using those sticks and equipment for years and years and years. Shit's expensive and in our neighbourhood no one has that kind of cash. We don't have that kind of cash for registration fees either, which is why our outdoor rink is bumping. None of the kids are off playing minor hockey. Our minor hockey is here, where we get to skate all we want. Technically, you're supposed to buy a community league membership, but no one has ever done that.

Charlie loves playing hockey and he plays fucking hard too. He's a staple in the annual cops-versus-neighbourhood game. I think they meant for the game to be for kids. But it's ended up that all the best players come out to really give it to the cops. It's the one chance all year you have to get your shots in and not get your skull split for it. There's no other circumstance where I would have seen Charlie smash down a cop, shoulder to chest, big *whoomph*, without him getting hammered back, cuffed and hauled off.

This hockey game is the highlight of the winter for a lot of people. And this year they decided to do the new rink revitalization grand announcement at the same time. Me, I can't play worth a damn but I've watched it every year since I was just a little guy. That was back when our mom was still around. She used to make Charlie take me everywhere. He would take me down to the outdoor rink from our rented duplex to sit in the makeshift bleachers and drink gallons of the free hot chocolate and McDonald's orange goop while he played. I'd have a cup in each hand long before we knew what the term *double fisting* meant. We're big hockey fans, Charlie and I. Someday I'd like to be able to watch the Oilers play live. That would be dope. Especially if we got good seats, but really I'd take anything. Charlie's mentioned that when he gets some cash together he's going to take me to one of the games.

The high school's Aboriginal student liaison, Doug, lets us watch Oilers games on the big projector screen they have in the student commons. Doug's a young guy from around here. He went through college or university, not sure which, and ended up back at the same school working with us shitbirds. Only reason I think he lets us go in to watch the games is because he doesn't have his own TV, or friends, so he gets company and a big-ass screen. Huge Oilers fan, that Doug. He's always got some piece of gear on, plus his bright-orange hat. A bunch of us guys from the neighbourhood wander over there to eat pizza, smash litres of root beer, Pepsi, and eat our weight in Doritos. Charlie comes by for the odd game, mainly the ones when he can't find anyone to drink beer with him. Doug doesn't mind that he comes by, even though he's long done with the high school. One time during a game, Doug and I were walking to grab the pizzas from the delivery guy. Doug had just finished paying for them and I was holding a stack of four piping-hot boxes when he turned to me and said, "You're finishing up grade ten this year, right?"

"Yup, just a couple more months," I answered.

"You doing alright with your grades?"

"Just missed the honour roll, by like one percent. My math teacher had it out for me."

"Sure, sure. What are you thinking of doing afterwards?"

"I don't know. Charlie's got a pretty good construction gig. Probably something like that."

"You ever think about university?" Doug asked.

"Nah, no money for that kind of thing. Wouldn't get in anyways."

"I wouldn't say never. You have a good head on your shoulders. We should get these pizzas downstairs before the guys start rioting. Anyways, you should think about it. We can talk more about it later if you want."

Later that night, after the Oilers finished getting their asses handed to them, Charlie and I were walking back toward Granny's. Charlie was smoking darts back to back. He used to time his walks by how many smokes he could power down. The high school to Granny's was a three-smoke walk. He had just finished his second when he turned to me.

"What were you and Doug talking about?" he asked.

"Not much, man, we were just waiting for the pizzas."

"You were gone a long time."

"Pizza took a while, delivery driver was stunned."

"That guy's not a creep to you or anything is he?" Charlie asked.

"No! Man, the guy was talking about university," I replied.

"I don't know. I knew that guy back in the day. He was only a few years ahead of me in school. I think he's into dudes."

"I think Doug's a pretty good guy."

"Never know, man, never know. Guy's gotta keep his head up."

They make all the Indigenous students have mandatory meetings with the guidance counsellor a few times a year. This is a different job at the school than the one Doug has. I read in one of the reports Granny has laying out on the kitchen table that they're supposed to work together to save us. Apparently, it's a combined effort to help us graduate from high school, as if this one-shoe-fits-all thing could ever work. Charlie's feet are twice the size of mine and he never finished shit.

"You sure you want to go to college?" The guidance counsellor asks me.

"Yup, broadcasting, or journalism, something like that," I reply. "Doug told me to start thinking of it."

"I think you'd be better off getting a trade than trying to do something like that." The guidance counsellor keeps playing with this golden cross necklace he's wearing. "Especially with your marks, you'd be a shoo-in for the welding or electrical program. You'd make great money. Could find a good wife, have some kids." He keeps going, keeps playing with the necklace, this weird little golden Jesus staring back at me. His top two shirt buttons are undone, letting the gold cross really reflect off his pasty white skin. "This isn't the time for dreams. It's time to really buckle down and think about being a productive member of society."

"I'll think about it, sir," I answer.

"Good. Here are the brochures from the Northern Alberta Institute of Technology."

"Can you get me one for the programs at MacEwan University?" I ask.

"Don't be a smartass. Just take welding. Kids like you shouldn't think too much about it."

"Think about what, sir?" I ask. He cringes a little bit every time I say *sir*.

"Life. If you could work on breaking out of the cycle you'd be doing good for yourself. For your family. That takes hard work though. Work that a career in the trades would help you with."

"Thank you, sir. You're absolutely right. I shouldn't think about university."

"I'm just saying a trade is the best way to go right now. And believe me, I know."

I want to ask him what it is he knows. The guy's been the guidance counsellor at the high school for probably thirty years. He looks it at least, with his big belly that sticks out over his pants. I wonder when the last time he saw his dick was.

"See you later, sir. Thank you for the advice," I reply. He nods at me and goes back to fingering his cross and staring at the computer screen. I didn't expect much from him; he's the same guy who told Charlie he'd be doing good if he stayed out of jail. If anyone was being a pedo it would be him for sure, not

Doug. A couple girls told me the guidance counsellor used to walk up and down the aisles in the classroom and rub his crotch along the sides of their desks. They noticed he always wore black pants, so they took to chalking up the sides of their desks, or putting gum on them, or marker, anything to start staining them. He'd be strolling around the school halls the rest of the day with all this shit all over his crotch. I don't think he even noticed.

Charlie and I have the same mom. Neither of us knew our dads, and we only knew our mom for a few years before she took off to Vancouver and left us at a group home until Granny came and got us. She feels like a shadow in my mind now. We used to get the odd message from her, a letter or a phone call saying she would be back to get us. I used to get all fired up every time one of the messages arrived. I'd start packing everything I had into an old Easton hockey bag and then looking up Vancouver and every picture I could find of it on the computers at school. Charlie would try and prevent me from getting so excited. "Just chill, little dude," he'd say. "Come and play some *Mario Kart* with me." When I wouldn't calm down, he'd start getting more frustrated. "Seriously, stop fucking packing. She isn't coming." He had that reality check burned into him. It took me a few more years to get there. Right around the same time that the messages stopped arriving.

"Come on man. Let's get out of here," Charlie says. We're hanging around MacEwan University. I bribed Charlie to come with me with a pack of smokes I found at a bus stop outside the 7-Eleven.

I'm sitting on a planter in some big common area. Charlie's got his black hoodie pulled up over his Cleveland Indians hat and he's pacing back and forth in front of me. Not going to lie, I'm pretty scared walking around in a place like this, and I thought having Charlie with me would make it a bit better. Guy has got skin like a bear but for some reason this place has him shrinking down to size.

"I don't like this place, man. Everyone's staring at us." He did have a point. "I'm sure we're one scared person away from security coming and chasing us out."

"What if I tell them I'm thinking of becoming a student here?" I ask.

"I dunno man, seems like they probably hear that all the time."

"We've got like fifteen minutes to go. Maybe we should head outside for a smoke?"

Charlie starts heading straight for the nearest doors. He runs straight into them, tries them again. "Fucking things are locked," he says. People are starting to notice us. They're not hiding their stares anymore.

"We'll go out the other ones."

"This place is stupid." Charlie lights his smoke up inside and starts speed walking toward the doors. The few people hanging around are now really looking at Charlie like he's injecting the second-hand smoke right into their lungs.

I'm about four steps behind Charlie coming out of the building when I hear the *bwoop bwoop*. Two quick sirens. Not too hard to figure out what kind of car that's coming from. Fuck me, someone probably called the cops on Charlie and me for being in the university. Then Charlie lit up that smoke, shit. I wish they had the same response time in the neighbourhood when something went down. I turn around and two cops are getting out of their car. These aren't the nice community empowerment cops who play hockey, these are the knuckleheads that they don't show on the news. They both swarm me before I can get going and throw me onto the ground. I look over and Charlie's running. He'll be long gone. I wish I was as fast as him.

"What, you drunk, kid? You shouldn't be trespassing," one of them says.

"How old are you anyways? You shouldn't have weed on you," the other cop says. I think to myself, *Are they seriously going to plant something on me, how clichéd are they?* I know to keep my mouth shut though.

"We got ourselves an underage trespassing drunk with a bunch of weed. You don't have any needles or anything on you, do you?"

"No sir," I answer. "No needles."

"Why are you drunk wandering around here, kid?"

"Not drunk, sir."

"Then why do you reek of booze? Why do you reek of weed? Come on, you mouthy little shit." The cop grabs me and slams me up against the car. He knees me right in the gut while he reaches to grab his cuffs. It knocks the wind out of me, and I'm huffing and wheezing, my lungs crawling for breath. He puts the cuffs on and yanks them way too tight, cutting off all the circulation to my hands.

"You ever been to juvie kid? Ah, who am I kidding, of course you fucking have," he says as he shoves me in the back of the cruiser.

When I was little I liked pretending to be the announcer for the annual cops-versus-neighbourhood hockey game on the outdoor rink. That's what got me interested in broadcast journalism. I grew up listening to 630 CHED Oilers fan radio with Rod Phillips. When other kids wanted a Comrie jersey or a Hemsky or something like that, I wanted a Phillips. I would stay up at night, radio dialled in, practising along with Rod. A couple of Granny's friends told me that someday I would be doing play-by-play for the Oilers games. When I heard that, I couldn't wait for the next game to be on so I could work on my skills. I couldn't imagine a better life than getting to go and watch hockey games for a living. Back then I was still young enough that I figured Charlie would end up in the NHL, and that someday I'd be announcing his name as he scored goals and fought people.

Turns out the cops are just campus peace officers. They drive me back to the other side of campus and chuck me in some sort of holding room. It looks just like the guidance counsellor's office. I wait in there for a couple hours while they dick around. I sit there and count the bricks on the wall. This would be a lot more entertaining if I really was high or drunk. Eventually they both come strutting in like they're king shits.

"We're going to be charging you with trespassing."

"Maybe next time you'll think twice about coming onto campus with your gangbanging buddies," one cop says.

"You dumb-ass, you thought you could just come here? You're lucky we didn't find anything on you or you'd be going away for a long time," the other cop says. "You're going to have to wait here a bit longer until city police show up to take you away."

Another hour goes by where I'm counting bricks and thinking. Charlie did a quick minute in the Young Offender Centre a year or two ago. It wouldn't be the worst. I'll probably have to finish my high school inside and definitely won't be going to university after. But fuck it. Worse things have happened to far better people. I'll be okay. It was just a matter of time until something like this went down anyways.

A city police officer enters the room. She stares at me. She's not saying anything. I keep my head down avoiding her eyes. Then she turns and walks out of the room, closing the door behind her.

"How old's that kid in there?" I hear her ask the rent-a-cops. The office is small enough that all their words are coming right through the crappy door.

"Old enough to be causing shit here," one of them says.

"What did he do again?" she asks.

"He was trespassing with one of his gang buddies who got away."

"He's definitely not in a gang. You know that right?" she asks.

"No, he is, he's Native and he was with another Native guy."

"You've never actually seen someone in a gang, have you?" I can hear the anger on her tongue. "So how old is he?"

"We haven't asked him for ID yet," one rent-a-cop says.

"Are you fucking kidding me?"

The door opens up and the city cop comes in flanked by the two campus peace officers. They stand by the door looking like they're about to beat the shit out of me if I try and run.

"How old are you?" She asks.

"Sixteen," I say.

"Why were you on campus?"

"It's open house night. I was thinking about going to school here, for journalism."

"You want to go to school here?" she asks. I shrug. Charlie always tells me don't say anything, they can use it against you later. I can feel the blood running back to my hands. I wish I had the same nerve that blood does, to just continue to move no matter what, to run until it can't run no more, to get up and leave. Charlie was right, this is stupid. Why did I ever think this was a good idea?

"We're pretty sure he's been drinking," one of the campus cops says. "We could probably charge him for that."

The city cop stares him down. "You can go check out the open house," she says.

I say nothing.

When they finally let me go, I weave through the campus filled with other kids my age. Most are with their parents, some are in friend groups, but they all have that same excited nervous buzzing energy to them. It stuns me. The fear that I felt walking onto the campus earlier with Charlie starts building up again. Outside the campus gates it's only a few blocks back toward the outdoor rink. I bet Charlie's waiting for me there.

3. BIKES

Alex was fresh out of rehab and I was fresh out of my second year of university when we crowned ourselves bike kings. While other students took off on parent-paid summer travels, started up summer jobs, or took up full-time hours at the bars and pubs, we started stealing bikes. We stole a lot of other stuff too, don't get me wrong. But we had the bike system down. Funny thing, my dream in life at that time was to work at a bookstore. The fear in the eyes of the uppity suburbia kids who accepted my resumé or application with shaking hands told me that was never going to happen. Even if that resumé somehow made it to a manager, they would see that classic Avenue of Champions address and throw it in the trash. I was well suited to bikes, though.

I'm crashing with my girlfriend, Ashley, and her mom in those old row townhouses just off the Avenue. They're shit. But they aren't walk-up apartment shit. At least in the row townhouses you don't have people living in the hallways of your building.

That's a walk-up apartment thing. Having to dodge the needles and sleeping bodies stacked up in the entryways and under the stairs. Ashley is taking classes at Inner City High. Her mom works the day shift at the 7-Eleven on the Avenue. So they get up and roll out around eight every morning. I haven't been allowed to be there by myself ever since I let some of my buddies come by and they emptied out all the cleaning supplies from the closet and the food from the fridge. It wasn't really my fault. I didn't know that Mike was back on pint. Never mind that the food is always only leftover chicken wings and taquitos from the Sev. But anyways, because of that I gotta clear out when they leave. Alex wakes up early too. He's keeping those rehab hours. Waking up early and doing some exercise, playing guitar, doing things that keep your mind busy, so you don't start huffing for breakfast kind of thing.

After I'm out of the house I wander by where Alex lives with his aunty. She's great, and usually has something for us to eat. She's a social worker in one of those downtown offices where they're always drinking tons of coffee. She brings the big Tim Hortons cardboard things home with her and Alex and I will help ourselves to the leftovers. Microwaved up the next morning with tons of cream and sugar, that's our style. I'm a double-double guy but Alex, that dude switched out coke for sugar.

We gotta be on the LRT before nine. The train cops start checking passes after that. Then we can also get to the university and keep an eye on the people leaving their bikes. The best ones are when you can tell that the person is going into work for the day. They're leaving that bike locked up outside and they're not going to be back for eight hours. We can be on our third or fourth run of the day at that point and their bike, well, that was sold three hours ago. Anyways, we set up shop at the university. I check the ashtrays for some halfies. Then we smoke those while we wait for a couple good bikes to roll up. Alex's got these big-ass cutters he borrows from his mechanic uncle. They'll snip any lock in one chomp. We got these nice backpacks to hide the cutters in. Beautiful big amiskwaciy Academy letters on the back of them with this nice black, red, white and yellow medicine wheel underneath. Real quality, you can tell, not like most of the promotional swag we used to get when we were on the poor kid's summer camp tours back when we were young.

We hit the High Level Bridge, swing through the fountains at the legislature grounds, cut down Jasper to Ninety-Fifth and then it's a straight shot north to Dave's house. Dave's this big white guy. He's covered in faded pen tattoos, definitely in and out of the remand. He's the kind of guy you don't want to mess with. He rips us off on the bikes. But fuck it. We don't have to deal with selling them or trying to pawn them off ourselves. Usually he gives us twenty-five bucks a bike, sometimes fifty if it's a really fancy new one, sometimes ten if it looks like it came from the tent camps in the River Valley. We don't go for the ten-dollar ones. Not our style. We need cash. Dave sells the bikes online, but not in Edmonton. He sells them in Saskatoon or Calgary. Then he gets one of his cronies to drive a whole bunch of them down there at once. Probably makes some good cash that way. I don't really care. I don't like Dave and don't want to be around him any more than I have to be. Something's off with him and I don't want to be there when he snaps.

After we deal with Dave then it's back to the LRT. Alex and I try to avoid train cops and we'll hop on and off the trains when we see them coming. We'll do that run three or more times depending on how we're feeling. Most days we end up walking away with one hundred each in cash. Sometimes we'll even stop in and visit Ashley on her lunch break from school. There are a couple other cuties she hangs out with there that I wouldn't mind talking to sometime. I try to convince Alex to chat one of them up but he's got other demons on his mind right now. Don't need to add on to that. I doubt that Ashley tells them we're bike kings. Not that we're qualified to do anything else. I mean I doubt I would make more working at a McDick's or sweeping floors or something. And besides, I get yelled at enough by rich people on campus all year. I don't need that during the summer too.

Ashley and her mom don't get along. Her mom thinks Ashley's going to be a doctor or a veterinarian or something and then support her. She spends all her time drinking boxed white wine and cruising million-dollar real estate listings and expensive furniture websites. By the time Ashley gets home from school her mom is liquored up and yelling about how ungrateful she is and how she ruined her life. It's just white noise to Ashley at this point. She's been hearing it since she was eight. I get mad though. If they weren't letting me crash there, I would tell Ashley's mom how I really feel about her dream of riding her daughter's coattails.

A few months later Ashley's mom will have a complete breakdown. She tries to stab Ashley and then takes off with some john who frequents the 7-Eleven on a regular basis after his late-night excursions. We won't be able to pay rent and Ashley'll have to move in with her cousin and I'll end up in a car in an alley by the university. But that's another story.

This one day Alex and I decide to keep bikes from our last run of the day. I've got this funny purple mountain bike with the handlebars already bent to shit and he's riding this BMX with pegs on only one side. We'll probably get twenty-five for the BMX but Dave ain't going to give us anything for that purple mountain bike. We're ripping around the hood on the bikes, killing time, looking for girls. It's one of those hot summer days where the city's just dead. All the schools are out but it's too hot for the kids to be in the parks. Too hot for the homeless boys and ladies to be wandering around. Just sinister heat. We decide to bike down to the legislature to go sit in the fountain. When we were kids Alex and I went to the day programming they ran on the Avenue for inner-city youth. They'd bring us down to the legislature fountain for us to swim around. It was the best. There's a couple of those groups of kids running around today. I try to pick out similar faces, finding the kid who I was, who Alex was, who Ashley was back in the day. Back before the reality of who we really were set in.

"You ever think of throwing one of these off the High Level Bridge?" I point with my lips toward the purple bike. We're sitting on the fountain ledge with our feet in the water. He's wearing jeans he cut into shorts and a black T-shirt with some local band's name on it. He dunks his head in the water for a couple seconds then pulls it back out, shaking his hair like a dog.

"I saw a guy whip a tire off the bridge once," Alex answers. "Not even a crew or nothing, just rolled this tire down from the south side. Got about halfway across then whipped it over the side. Buddy didn't even watch it land, just turned around and started walking back."

"Granny told me once someone jumped and got hung up in those wires underneath. Took them a while to get him untangled," I say.

"That one guy from high school, fuck, what was his name? He jumped, remember?" Alex said. "Greg or something like that I think. I dunno."

In the background a group of people in fancy suits, must be politicians, are walking around the outside of the legislature building. They're all laughing and shaking hands with each other. You can see their pasty skin, devoid of any summer sun, reflecting off the legislature fountain water.

"You ever think you're going to end up like them, Daniel?" Alex nods toward the group.

"Fuck no, man, how would that happen?" I reply.

"Well you being in university and all seems like a good start."

"Man, only reason I'm in school is I'm riding that Children's Services funding. Soon as they quit paying my tuition, it's over. I'm out. Shit's expensive."

"I got more chance ending up like Greg then I got ending up like them," Alex says. He spits on the ground toward where the group of suits are saying goodbye to each other. We're far enough away that they don't notice. The security guard walking around does though. He starts walking toward us with that *I'm going to smash your head in* swagger.

"Shit let's get out of here," I say. "I don't want to deal with this today."

Biking back up through downtown, we swing down 104th Street. There are a bunch of Lamborghinis, Ferraris and other rich cars. They're lining the block. I've never seen so much money in one place. All these men are standing outside the cars, smoking and bullshitting with each other. Even their clothes and shoes are screaming, "Steal me! He can replace me but I'll pay your rent for the year." Alex and I get off our bikes and start walking them beside all the shine. I swear you can see cash reflecting from the downtown buildings onto the paint of these things. The men don't pay attention to us. We're walking by the last car, this red Ferrari. I'm a couple steps behind Alex. I watch as his eyes cloud over a bit and he picks up the BMX he's riding and smashes one of the pegs into the Ferrari's windshield and the other peg into the door. The car window shatters and the other peg scratches up the paint.

"What the fuck!" someone yells behind us. Alex's already pulled the BMX back from the door hopped on and taken off. I get on mine and I'm following behind him. "Hey kid, get back here!" someone's screaming now from behind us. But we're gone. We've been running our whole lives. Ripping back behind the homeless shelters and onto the walking path that runs along the LRT tracks. Through the hole in the fence that some boys cut out to make a shortcut for their bottle depot runs, back past the pawn shops and liquor stores, and down the Avenue. At some point we can hear sirens but those could be the sirens for a million different things around here.

4. THE BAKE SALE

Granny watched as Daniel bounded off the bus, walked up to the fence that surrounded her porch and hopped over it, as you would jump over the boards in a hockey rink. As he landed, he plucked a bright-red cherry tomato from her plant, one of the last of the year, and ate it in one bite.

"Granny, shit, sorry I'm late," Daniel said, as he sat down in the old red-faded-to-pink rocking chair that her late husband used to sit in. "I got caught up for a beer after class with Alex and ended up coming straight here from the U." He stood up as abruptly as he'd sat down, walked over and grabbed a Pilsner out of the fridge. "You want a beer?" he asked her.

"namoya, I have one going," Granny replied, pointing with her lips to a plastic glass filled up with Clamato and beer.

"I'm not going to lie. One of the best things about Grandpa being dead is that the beer is cold now," Daniel said.

"That was an old army thing. They never drank cold beer back in the day. He could never get used to it."

"Just warm piss, eh? You want to order food or head over to the pub? I think there might be a band playing tonight or something."

"Let's go to the pub. I've been sitting in here all day."

The pub was half a block away. Closer to her apartment than the dining hall where most of the seniors in her assisted living building ate, if you counted it out foot by foot. She knew this because Daniel had paced it out one time after a few drinks of crabapple bounce. It was a drinkers' pub. The kind with a plaque devoted to regulars who had passed on over the years. And since it was basically attached to the seniors building she lived in, they needed a couple plaques, as they kept steadily filling up with names as people passed on.

"Pitcher of Canadian," Daniel called out to the server, a young beautiful nehiyaw lady who looked like she must be related to one of the Cardinal families from Saddle Lake. The server smiled at Daniel. Definitely a Cardinal, Granny figured. Back when the boys were younger and everyone lived in the house off the Avenue of Champions, the running joke was that if you threw a rock up in the air on the Avenue it would land on a Cardinal.

"You want a pizza, or what you thinking?" Daniel asked.

"I think I'm going to go with the lasagna."

"Oh man that sounds good too."

The server brought the jug of Canadian back and filled up two glasses for them. Granny wasn't sure how the server managed to keep her long black hair out of the beer. Granny had never had that same shine and thickness to her hair that the server did. It had always been short and curly, and then even more so when she permed it out during the seventies and eighties. That hair the server had, now *that* was hair to be envious of. Daniel thanked the server and she winked at him before returning to take the order of two old crusties hammering away on VLTS in the corner. The server came back after the crusties dismissed her with waves of unlit cigarettes.

"Shit, I'm sorry. I forgot to take your food order," the server said.

"A lasagna for my beautiful kohkom and I'll have some hot wings," Daniel replied.

"Psht, don't listen to this little shit. He only calls me kohkom when he's trying to impress a beauty like you with his university Cree," Granny said.

The server started laughing. She pulled out a chair and sat down with them. "Oh I'd tune his moniyaw ass up, don't worry," she said with a smile. She refilled their glasses even though they were only about half empty.

"Whoa, whoa, whoa, Métis you know," Daniel replied. "I'm a legit Lac Ste. Anne Bois-Brûlé ready to ride the buffalo hunts."

"Actually, you're right, he has spent too much time in university," the server laughed. "I'll go put your orders in. Let me know when you want more beer."

As she left, Granny reached over and swatted her boy on the head. "You smarten up and be nice to her. I think I know her family." They both laughed and took big gulps of their beers.

"You know, did I ever tell you the story of when Grandpa and I came here last?" Daniel said. She had heard it but she didn't mind listening again if he wanted to tell it.

"We were back at the apartment. It was when you and Irene took off to Prince Albert on the bus to visit the casino and I came up to stay with Grandpa. Anyways, we're sitting around drinking a beer, watching baseball, when he looks up at me and says, 'What do you say, a couple bachelors like us go grab something to eat and a beer?' Of course I said, 'Hell yeah, that sounds fun.' So I tell Grandpa to go put his coat on, I'm gonna take a piss. I get out of the washroom and he's standing there, full coat on, toque, ready to roll. He looks up at me and says, 'Where are we going again?' So I say, 'The pub, let's roll.' We do the usual slow, slow, slow, slow walk over as he takes his time checking everything out even though it's like twenty below out." Her boy stopped to drink the last of the beer in his cup. He caught the eye of the server behind the bar and pointed at the empty pitcher. She winked back at him.

"So, anyways, we get in and sit down. Same server actually. And we order up a few beers and some food. Do you remember Alex's ex-girlfriend?"

"The nurse?"

"Yeah, the nurse. So his girlfriend is in here with a whole bunch of her nursing friends. Just all drop-dead gorgeous women, you know. And I know a few of them from parties. Anyways, they come over and sit down with us. I look over at Grandpa and he's all like, hell yeah this is awesome. So we're surrounded by beautiful women, drinking beers, having wings, just the best time, you know."

The server came back with a pitcher of beer. She filled up the empty glasses and then sat down with them. Daniel kept going with his story.

"So at the end of the night he motioned to the server and said bring us our bill."

"Was this with your Grandpa?" the server asked.

"Yeah. So anyways he says bring us our bill." Granny's boy smiled at the server. "And Grandpa goes, 'Let me get this one.' He pulls out his wallet, grabs a five-dollar bill out and throws it on top of the pub bill. Now, we had drunk at least three pints each plus all the food. Our bill was definitely north of fifty. So I say to him, 'I'll pay it.' So I grab his five bucks and walk up to pay at the counter. Tipped incredibly well, too, if I remember."

"You definitely didn't," the server said.

"Like at least 25 percent I'm sure." Both Granny and the server roll their eyes and look at each other. "So, best part is I get back to the table. Grandpa has his coat on, all ready to go, and he looks at me and says, 'You get any change?' Luckily I had a couple coins in my pocket so I tossed him two loonies. He pocketed them and we rolled on back."

"How's your grandpa doing?" the server asked.

"He's dead."

"Well, I'd better go see if your food is ready."

After supper, at Granny's apartment, they settled into their spots in front of the TV. The Jays are up nine to five against the Rays in the top of the ninth. Only a couple outs left. They finish the game out.

"Well, should we see how they're doing? And what we can get?" Daniel asked.

"Sounds good to me." They stand up and walk into the bedroom that Grandpa used to sleep in.

"Oh shit, these look beautiful, Granny. You have the touch." Two rows of marijuana plants in planters under lights ran the length of the bedroom. "Oh hell yeah."

"We can get way more this way. They've grown a lot in the last week," Granny said.

"Yes. Yes. We can. Beats the couple plants we had going in the storage closet."

Granny had always been a moonshiner. She was raised by her kohkom, OG, Original Granny as Daniel put it, on the road allowances north of St. Paul. Her mushum had passed away when he was in his early twenties, from one of the diseases that ripped through the Prairies. Her OG kohkom had to support a large family and she moonshined. She moonshined hard and made enough money to survive and raise her family as a single Métis lady. Granny moved in with her sometime around her tenth or twelfth birthday, and had to help with the moonshining. When Granny moved to the city back when she was in her teens, she kept making hooch. No one had extra money and hooch, shine, bounce, was always appreciated in any form. She could make some good extra coin on the side by slinging shine and she had good recipes.

As the booze started flowing more freely it became harder and harder to make money selling moonshine. Eventually she only made it recreationally. She never made any money off it anymore, but she kept going because that's all she ever knew, and it was a link back to her own childhood and her OG kohkom. Then Daniel convinced her to switch from moonshining to growing and selling weed instead. Not that she needed much convincing, she knew that she wasn't making money anymore and an old army pension wasn't much to live on. Daniel couldn't sell the hooch at university; it was more of a novelty, and all her friends and family had been dying off for years. She was also hoping she could make enough to move out to Vancouver Island and get away from the apartment, where the memory of her husband hung around and the winters drove her body indoors for months on end.

"So, what can I take?" Daniel asked.

Granny pulled two old four-litre ice cream pails off the shelves and passed them over to Daniel. He cracked the lids on both. They were stuffed to the top with fresh buds. He took a big whiff and emptied them both into his backpack, which was lined with a garbage bag.

"This looks like Métis Mindfuck to me," Daniel said. "Think that name will sell?"

"Whatever you say," Granny said.

"Perfect. This is a lot. We'll get some good cash for this."

"Do you have my money from the last haul?" Granny asked.

"Yup, right here." Daniel pulled out a green sour-cream-and-onion Pringles container from the water bottle holder on his backpack. He pulled a couple chips off the top and then emptied out a wad of rolled-up bills. He placed the chips back in the container and passed the wad to Granny. "All you."

Granny had always appreciated that about Daniel. He wasn't the kind of kid who saw a necessity for money and was more than happy to turn it all over to her. His tuition was paid by a bursary for children who had lived in group homes, and he just asked her for enough to get by. Her husband had been the same when he was alive. He wanted nothing to do with money and let her run the show when it came to all financial matters. She pulled out a couple hundred bucks from the wad and looked up at Daniel.

"I'm still good from last time. It's all you, Granny." He shrugged. "I'm going to hit up the bus back before the late-night riff-raff gets into the station." Daniel walked over and wrapped Granny up in a big hug. She watched as he left the way he entered, eating a cherry tomato and hockey-boy-hopping over the railing of her balcony.

Granny missed moonshine. Weed was easy; it didn't take the work and discipline that moonshine did. You didn't have to create and perfect a recipe that worked with the system you had in place. You could just grow a couple plants, snip the buds, dry them out for a few weeks and then send them with your boy back down to the university for cash. There was no art to it. At least none that she cared to create. Weed was going to sell no matter what, so no point getting all fancy-schmancy. Moonshine, though, that was art. Every recipe differed depending on what the ingredient was that was going to carry it. But at the same time, there was a process you needed to follow or it would all go to hell. She missed the smells of yeast and fermenting bread coming off the stills and floating on the wind into the cabin she lived in when she was a kid. She missed watching OG kohkom get excited as she tapped three times on the jars to get the proof. She missed bringing old jugs full of hooch up to the local dances and the sounds of the cheers when they arrived. You would never get that same reaction from marijuana.

Daniel hated the bus. It just took so long. If people ever came on that he could talk to, or if something interesting happened, that would be alright. But it never came up. If it was interesting, it was usually just some drunk yelling. Pretty girls never rode the bus. At least the ones from his courses at the university didn't. Most of them, he imagined, lived close by, rode nice, fancy bikes with baskets on the front, or drove nice-ass cars. The girls on the bus were the girls he had known forever, or at least the same type. They had big, pouffed-out hair, wore black hoodies and would beat the shit out of him if he so much as looked at them the wrong way. Daniel wanted to meet someone who might offer him a glimpse into a life he didn't know. One that didn't necessarily involve being stuck in the dingy-ass walk-up apartments on the Avenue of Champions.

Last year, he went on some dates with a woman from the west side whose dad was some managing partner in a big-shot law firm. They met in an Indigenous studies course at the beginning of his third year of university. Daniel had run his mouth to the professor about Métis getting a bum rap. After class, the woman came up to Daniel and told him she really appreciated what he had said. She told him her dad was the main lawyer for the *Blackstone* TV show and she was part Métis because her great-great-great-great-grandfather was Cherokee. They drank a bunch at the campus bar and then continued the party for a few more nights at Daniel's apartment before parting ways. Daniel borrowed his buddy Alex's aunty's car to drop her off. He had never seen a house that big. Just these massive-ass bricks everywhere, and white arches. He told the woman that usually people like him got shot if they pulled into the driveways of houses like this.

"Don't be silly," she said. They never hung out again. He pestered her a few times for a drink after class but she always had an excuse. Alex told him she just wanted to check out the Avenue of Champions intimately, or get back at some Audi-driving law-school boyfriend.

"What'd you expect?" Alex asked as Daniel moped around. "For the two of you to live happily ever after? She'd move you into her daddy's big-ass house and he'd give you some cushy-ass office job? Give your head a shake buddy."

Daniel's roommate was never home. She spent most of her time either working at a hospital on the south side or at her boyfriend's place out in Pembina Creek. This didn't bother Daniel at all. He liked the solitude when he got home. He didn't have to worry about interrupting anyone or about anything going down. And no one got mad at Alex and him when they would be up all night drinking beers and playing nineties rock songs on their guitars.

Daniel got off the bus at the giant baseball bat and walked the block to his apartment. "Why don't you just slide…" Daniel could hear Alex singing as he got closer. Alex usually climbed up onto the second-storey balcony and let himself in through the sliding door if no one was around. He made the same entrance when people were around too. He lived with his aunt and uncle a couple blocks away, but they both worked off-hours, his uncle at the bus depot and his aunt as a youth worker. In their tiny old bungalow you couldn't play guitar, be loud or drink a bunch of beers except for Fridays when it was fucking *on* until they took off to the Mona Lisa Pub on the Avenue. Daniel could see a couple homeless guys, ho-bros as he and Alex called them, shooting up in the entryway of the apartment building. Instead of interrupting them, Daniel jumped up, grabbed the bars of the balcony railing and pulled himself up, then went in the sliding door just as Alex had earlier. There was no point in locking the door. If someone wanted to come in, they would no matter what, and they usually smashed the glass, which meant blood everywhere.

"Foo Fighters? Nice, buddy." Daniel grabbed a couple Pilsners out of the case that Alex had left in the fridge.

"Dave Grohl, my dude. Guy slays." Alex took one of the beers and set it beside the one he already had.

"You get paid or something? What's with the fancy shit?"

"On special. How's Granny?" Alex asked.

"Granny's Granny. Just growing and watching baseball. I should really go up there more," Daniel replied.

"Man, you go up there like twice a week, that's quite a bit. All my grandparents are long dead yo."

"Granny told me she can't die until she's ninety-three. Cause that's when her granny and her sisters and her mother and all the women in our family die apparently."

"I'll be lucky if I make twenty-seven," Alex said.

"Shit man, I'm lucky that I made twenty-two."

Daniel picked up the other acoustic guitar and they played a few songs, switching from Foo Fighters to Eagle-Eye Cherry, then Gaslight Anthem and then a couple of Alex's own creations. They went through the case of Pilsner and then weighed out weed into eighths and quarters. None of the kids at the university ever bought in larger quantities than that. A couple months back Daniel had used some of their profits to buy a vacuum sealer, which worked well to retain the flavour and freshness of the buds. It also gave Granny and him a bit of a signature to their product as they would write the amount and the name on the sealed baggie. For a while there when Daniel was really into his Cree language course at the U, he would write the names in syllabics. But the translating got hard, especially with a name like Métis Mindfuck—what would you do with that?

On Wednesdays, the free shuttle bus came to Granny's building and whisked all the white-hairs away to the River Cree Casino on Enoch. The casino gave each person who rode the shuttle a lunch voucher, five dollars in poker chips and a gift. Granny wasn't the gambler that her friends were, never had been, but each week she took the bus anyways. It was a good excuse to get out of the building and the casino reminded her of a younger time when you could still smoke everywhere and be surrounded by other Métis and Cree people. She always got to the shuttle lineup early so she could get a window seat.

The city had grown right around Enoch. Back when her brother first moved out there, Granny and her family would walk or hitchhike out to visit him. They used to have to go down country roads for hours. Now it was straight suburbs. Houses that could have fit twenty of the tiny one-room shacks she was raised in inside their square footage. Her brother had passed away a few years earlier. He was buried in the Enoch graveyard. When he was on his deathbed and Granny went to visit him, he told her that he wanted his body placed in a tree in the Rocky Mountains. None of this cemetery shit. His family thought that might be a bit improper, so he ended up in a grave right under a big cross just off the highway that pipelines through the reserve.

Granny's friend Morene always sat next to her on the shuttle bus. The two of them met right when Granny and her husband had first moved back to the city after years in Saskatchewan. They were neighbours in the building, and Morene was Cree from Loon Lake, Saskatchewan. She didn't know a word of the language, or at least claimed not to as many people of Granny's generation did, but they still had that shared history, something Granny could never have with the settlers. Morene liked to gamble. Nothing big, just playing the penny slots, but it was still fun to watch the excitement she got from a good win. Her white curls would be bobbing up and down, starting to bounce faster and faster as she sensed a good pull coming on. The people-watching entertained Granny more than anything else. Granny didn't think too much about a big win. She had never really won anything in her life. This wasn't going to be the place to start that. But every once in a while the idea crossed her mind. All she needed was enough money to move out to Vancouver Island and live for another thirteen years. How much would cover that? Fifty thousand? If she was daydreaming, she may have tacked on another twenty-five to give to Daniel. He said he didn't want it now, but he might later.

Today at the River Cree, Granny headed straight to the breakfast spot. Four dollars for anything on the menu and unlimited coffee. She was a big bacon-and-eggs lady, the classics, none of this eggs Benedict bullshit. That was for rich people, even if it did cost the same amount. Morene went right to the slots and they made a plan to meet up for lunch around 11:45 to beat the rush. As she was eating her over-easy eggs, she listened in to the conversation a couple RCMP officers were having at the table next to her.

"I heard if that Trudeau loser gets elected, they're gonna legalize weed."

"Bullshit man, no way that's gonna happen."

"What, that they'll legalize it?"

"Nah, that he'll get elected. Who the fuck votes Liberal?"

"Not me, that's for damn sure. This country is already going to shit with all the Syrians coming in. Let alone if they legalize weed. Can only imagine."

"I'll move to the States for sure."

"Can you imagine looking outside and everyone's smoking weed? Boom, everyone will be a lazy fuck in no time. Just munching out and not doing a day's work."

Granny had heard enough. She had tuned them out before the inevitable racism kicked in. Weed getting legalized though. What would that actually mean? And what would that mean for her and Daniel? She'd have to ask him next time he came to visit. But the cops were probably right. Who the fuck votes Liberal? Granny tried to steer clear of politics; nothing good came from getting mixed up in the affairs of others. She pushed the politics talk to the back of her head. The runny yolks on her plate were starting to harden and she wouldn't have to think of any of that if she got the right pull on the slots.

Things were a lot easier back in the moonshine days. Except that one time when her Uncle Jimmy shot the RCMP officer. That didn't end well for anyone. Weed though, this was a whole new thing and so far Daniel was right, it had been bringing in the money that they needed.

Granny found her friend Morene sitting with a crew of other ladies from the building. Morene had tipped a chair over on the VLT beside her. "I was wondering if you were going to come. It's getting harder and harder to hold this. Ladies kept coming up and asking about it," Morene said. "Apparently it's hot."

Granny looked around. A bunch of the white-hairs were staring daggers at her. She shrugged her shoulders and pulled the chair back and sat down. "Fuck 'em," she said. Morene started laughing at her brazen swearing. "What, you never heard language like that back in the bush?" Granny continued, asking with a smile.

"Oh, we heard all that language and more. I just forget about it sometimes. I might need to go to church when I get back."

Morene and Granny both went to Sacred Heart Church. Granny wasn't particularly religious, but she liked Sacred Heart because the pastor brought the drums in and smudged before Mass. She didn't get enough of that in her life and that place was one of the few where she could recognize the old songs from the drummers. She didn't get that at the round dances Daniel would drag her too.

"You think they're ever going to legalize marijuana?" Granny asked Morene.

"Now why would they do something silly like that?" Morene answered.

* * *

"Does anyone have any thoughts on why we need to look at history from an Indigenous perspective?" The professor asked. Daniel slunk farther down in his chair in the back of the university lecture hall. The worst thing about the fourth-year seminar Native studies courses was that there were only twenty-five students or less in each class. It made it hard to hide. Whereas in the larger general courses you could slink into the back of the lecture hall—or not even show up—and no one would notice.

"So we can create an equal voice for Indigenous historical perspectives?" one of the keener students from the front row asked.

"Precisely," the prof replied. He had introduced himself at the beginning of the year as an uninvited guest to Treaty Six territory, of Irish and American descent, born and raised in Boston. He was honoured to be on the ceded territories of the Métis, Nakota Sioux, Cree, Dene, Anishnabe, Saulteaux... He kept droning on.

"I wonder if he realizes the irony in that?" Keesha whispered to Daniel. Keesha and Daniel sat next to each other in most classes. She lived out on Enoch and dominated any class lecture, when she chose to that is.

"I wish you were teaching this course," Daniel whispered back. "I'd fucking pay attention then."

"Daniel, anything to add to the discussion?" The prof asked.

"Nope," Daniel replied. "Well, maybe you should refer to the Métis as God's chosen people?" The class laughed.

"Remember, class, that participation makes up a significant part of the grade for third- and fourth-year courses in the department," the prof said, while staring directly at Daniel. I wonder if he wants to buy some weed, Daniel thought.

Daniel hated university. Nothing about it felt right for him. Back when he was in high school, he wanted to take journalism at MacEwan and be a sports reporter. Then in his last year, the Aboriginal student liaison at his high school convinced him that with his grades, he should go into Native studies. Daniel realized that at least the career path might be more interesting. He could already see the government recruiters chomping at the bit to hire Métis and First Nations students with Native studies degrees. They did recruitment fairs at the university all the time to hire interns in various provincial or federal ministries. All the profs talked all the time about how good these jobs were. Keesha told Daniel once that she thought it was all some big conspiracy to try to keep First Nations and Métis people down by giving them entry-level positions. They would never give one of these people a job in a leadership position, though, and then they could get off telling the rest of Canada to look at all these good, gainfully employed Natives, reconciliation must really be working, yada yada yada. Daniel trusted Keesha's opinion over the profs'.

Class ended and Daniel stood up to leave.

"You want to come to the First Peoples' House?" Keesha asked him. "A couple of us are going to do beadwork with the Elder."

"Pass today, sorry, I gotta go and do some writing." That was always Daniel's excuse. Keesha would invite him to participate in different protests, cultural activities, political events and he always told her he had to write.

"All good, see you tomorrow," she said. Daniel knew she didn't buy the writing thing. But he had made the mistake of drinking a couple beers before class and telling her all about his dreams of being a poet like Leonard Cohen. "You should be more like Tenille Campbell," she had told him in response. But now at least he had the writing thing as an excuse.

Instead, Daniel ended up at Dewey's, the University of Alberta's campus arts bar, which had a great hidden upstairs lounge area that no one went to except the odd couple looking for a spot to make out. He ordered a beer and headed up to a table in the lounge. He sat down and laid out his textbooks and laptop so that anyone who did come up would think he was just another student studying.

"Hey man." One of the students he sold to came up and sat down across from him.

"Check out this reference." Daniel slid a massive old psychology textbook across the table. Inside, he had cut out a square in the pages so he could fit a bag of weed. The student put the book in his bag, opened it so the ziplocked weed bag fell into it, then he put the money back in the textbook and slid it back across.

"Reference looks great. I think I'll use it, but I might need a new one next week," the student said. He stood up and left.

"Just text me first," Daniel replied.

Another student client came up five minutes later, then another one, then another one. Daniel usually arranged them five minutes apart, but every once in a while one showed up early or late. It didn't matter, they were all there to get weed.

One time, Alex had accompanied Daniel to Dewey's while he sold. Alex thought the whole process was ridiculous. "Dude, why'd you create such an elaborate system. It's so unnecessary. Just fucking meet people in bathroom stalls or something, I don't know," Alex had said.

"It's better this way. University dorks fucking think it's gangster. Makes them think they're doing something badass."

"Man, if you were actually dealing something real and did this, they would kick the shit out of you," Alex said.

"Good thing it's just weed then."

Daniel drank a couple more pints of flat house lager while he finished selling the stash he had brought that day. The beer was almost on the level where he needed to mix the first couple pints with orange juice to cut that shitty leftover taste out of the cup. But not quite, so he just grimaced through the first couple until his palate adjusted. His connection network for selling ran strong, mainly resulting from word of mouth. Most of the students he sold to would never want to approach a real drug dealer. That would be too out of their comfort zone. So an easy way to still get weed was this university hookup. Daniel tried to play the part up a bit. But most of the actual dealers he knew were complete burnouts who welcomed any excuse to show off their weird possessions to any new person who came by their apartment. The number of snakes, weird fish, ninja swords and other paraphernalia him and Alex had had to look at over the years would have filled any museum devoted to the art of being a sketchball.

Daniel was feeling good when he rolled out of the pub and hopped on the train back up to the Avenue. Something about a few pints, an empty backpack and a pocket full of cash gave him an extra boost of confidence. Enough that he didn't notice the group of kids getting on the platform at the stop before his. He didn't notice them get off at the next stop and start following him down the Avenue. When they caught up to him outside the station, he realized he was fucked.

"Yo man, you got a smoke?" This large kid, maybe fifteen or sixteen but the size of a big hockey player, was the one who came up and asked him. He had a black Chicago Blackhawks toque on and it was pulled down low, his hoodie pulled up over that. The other kids in the group, about four of them, hung back. They all had a similar look going. Daniel knew it all too well. He tried to place the kid, maybe he knew him or one of his cousins, but got nothing.

Daniel took off running. *Fucking beers*, he thought. He could feel the confidence gone, replaced by a cold fear, and the beers were sloshing in his gut. He made it to the edge of the parking lot before the kid caught up with him. He tackled Daniel into a bus stop bench on the side of the street. Daniel could feel his arm stretch and then snap with the landing. The kid's friends had caught up and they started kicking Daniel. Each blow landed harder than the last, until finally he stopped feeling any of them. Daniel knew there was blood leaking out underneath him but he didn't know how much. He couldn't get up. He could feel the backpack getting torn off him and someone going through his pockets. *I hope they don't stab me*, he thought before blacking out.

Granny received the message later that night that Daniel had been rushed to the hospital. She was off playing crib in Irene's apartment after their supper. Granny had a feeling something must have been up because she was getting really good cards.

74

If you receive hand after hand of fours, fives and sixes and cuts of the same to make twenties and twenty-fours all the time, the balance is off. Something must have happened to throw off the balance, but she pushed that out of her head. Irene thought it was weird too. Usually they broke even on their games, but that night Granny had skunked Irene three times. When Granny got back to her apartment, she saw the red flash on her phone indicating voicemails. She checked them. The first one was from Daniel's friend Alex. He said that Daniel had been hurt and he was on his way to the Royal Alex, but not to worry, it should all be good. The next was from someone at the Royal Alex saying that her grandson had been admitted. The next one was from a city cop asking her to call him back and gave a phone number. She deleted all of them and definitely didn't write down the cop's phone number.

Granny didn't trust hospitals. When she was a little kid back in the bush, anyone who went to a hospital didn't come back. If they did, they were messed up and worse off than they had been when they left. She still believed in the land. If everyone in her family had lived into their hundreds before hospitals, then something must have gone wrong when Europeans came and started building them. Granny walked to her closet and pulled out a pair of mitts. They had been made out of a moosehide that her brother's wife at the time had tanned out on Enoch. The mitts had an elaborate flower pattern beaded on them: yarrow leaves stretching into rosehips, stretching into dandelions and underneath, layers of patches that she had sewn on over the years when her husband was still alive and had used them as his hunting mitts. Granny wished she could remember exactly what it was that each medicine did. She knew they told a story, and she knew the basics. If only her own granny was still alive; she had been able to create what was needed to heal anyone from the plants and animals around her. When Granny was a young girl, she would walk through the woods, helping gather what her own granny had needed. They built it on a case-by-case basis. You never took more than what you needed.

Granny poured herself a whisky and settled in to watch the evening news and then the sports highlights. She knew she wouldn't sleep that night. Sleep never came easy, and she felt an ache in her ribs that she knew was Daniel's pain transferring to her. Outside her front apartment window, a couple magpies were perched on the balcony railing, taking in the last light from the setting fall sun. Tomorrow she'd call Daniel's brother Charlie and get more details.

Daniel woke up in a morphine daze. Everything was foggy and he felt light. He looked down and saw a cord running out of his dick, and bandages all over him. His arm was also hooked up to an IV. He tried to sit up but the bandages wrapped around his middle prevented him from moving. A nurse walked by, noticed he was awake and came into the room. The nurse didn't look much older than Daniel, had tattoos running up and down his arms and one of those man-bun haircuts.

"Where'd you get your eagle done?" Daniel asked.

"Ha, on Whyte," the nurse said, deflecting the question. "How're you feeling?"

"Like a million bucks. When can I get out of here?" Daniel answered.

"Not for a bit. Your ribs and right arm are broken, you have a concussion and you have some internal bleeding happening. A doctor will be coming by shortly to tell you more about it. There are also a couple police officers here who will come by to chat with you."

"Figured. Did I get shanked?" Daniel asked.

"No, so consider yourself lucky." The nurse looked at the machine hooked up to Daniel, wrote something down on a chart and then walked out of the room.

"I should get an eagle tattoo." Daniel's morphine haze voice spoke out to the empty hospital room and he thought he could hear a coyote calling in the background. He slipped back into sleep.

He woke back up and could feel the pain this time. Daniel winced hard and started hyperventilating.

"We need you thinking clearly, son." An older cop with a stereotypical moustache was sitting beside him. A younger cop, who was trying for the moustache, was standing in the doorway. "They'll give you painkillers in a bit. Can you answer some questions for me?"

Daniel didn't say anything.

"Do you know who did this to you?"

"Nope," Daniel replied.

"Do you remember what they looked like?" He asked.

"Not at all. I couldn't see anything."

The cop in the doorway stared daggers at Daniel.

"You realize we're here to help you," the younger one said.

The older cop shot the younger one a look.

"So there's nothing you can give me?" He asked Daniel again.

"Sorry, no."

"Are you in a gang?" the cop asked Daniel.

"Ha, do I look like I'm in a gang?" Daniel responded. He knew what the cops were trying to do. They'd swing this around on him and start threatening him unless he gave something to them.

"Look, they jumped me from behind, I didn't see shit."

"Is your brother named Charlie?" the older cop asked.

"Yes," Daniel answered.

"He's got a bit of a record, hasn't he?"

Daniel shrugged.

"Is he in a gang?"

Daniel didn't move or say anything.

"Well, if you start remembering, let us know." The older cop placed a card on the bedside table beside Daniel. The younger one was still staring daggers at him. They turned and left.

Daniel started pressing the nurse call button. The same guy from earlier came in and drugged him up. He could feel the morphine cruising through his body and he fell back into sleep while coyotes howled all around him.

* * *

"Hey, Granny? How're you doing?" Charlie said.

"You heard?" Granny replied. She could feel the reverberations of Charlie's deep voice. He sounded, looked and acted like a bear most of the time. He could have been half-bear for all Granny knew, as no one had ever figured out who Charlie's father was.

"What you think?" Charlie growled.

"Do you know who it was?" Granny asked.

"Some little high school shits trying to be tough. Don't worry, they'll get theirs," Charlie said. "I know the one kid's cousin. They're all pretty new to the city here. One of the dumb-asses answered Daniel's phone when we called it."

"Make sure you get my money, too," Granny replied.

"Always, Granny."

She and Charlie didn't have the same relationship that she and Daniel did. By the time Charlie came to live with her, he was already a young man, wise to the city world and doing his own thing. Daniel on the other hand had been a big Granny's boy. Charlie would be gone all day and night, running around with his friends on the Avenue. Daniel would be hanging off her leg and her every move, following her around the house. They would read stories together and play pirate ships with Daniel's Lego, as well as *Mario Bros.* and *Duck Hunt* on an old original Nintendo that Granny had been given years ago. Granny was a deadeye shot. Rather than playing, Daniel would pretend to be the dog and run around, pretending to pick up the ducks that Granny was shooting on the screen. While they did this, Charlie would be drinking beer in the old rickety garage behind their house with his friends. The garage's roof was almost falling in, and you could open and close the door by simply lifting it up. People from the alley would often sleep in the garage or use it as a spot to shoot or smoke up. So nothing was stored in there except for a few old chairs that Charlie and his buddies would sit on, and the beer cans that they would leave, which would always be gone by dawn the next morning.

Grandpa had to go back to work during those years. He had been forced into early retirement from the military and had taken to spending every day hunting or fishing. He would be gone for weeks at a time on extended fishing trips, and then in the fall, extended hunting trips. Sometimes he would take Daniel along. Most of the time he went by himself though, or with his one friend. When Charlie and Daniel came to live with Granny, that all ended. They could get by on their military pensions themselves but with two boys, means were stretched thin. Grandpa's friend got him a job at the hide-tanning factory. It was long hours, but he didn't mind because he got to see the condition and quality of all the furs coming in from the trap-lines up north. Beautiful wolf, coyote, beaver, lynx pelts. He loved them all and loved seeing that that lifestyle still existed in the remote reaches of the province.

Grandpa kept a running tally of what areas the best hides were coming from. Sometimes at night, when they lay in bed under a homemade quilt, he'd talk to Granny about saving up, buying some traps and establishing a line. He didn't believe in government permits, he believed in animals and how they were the best indicator that everything would be well no matter how hard it got in the city. Granny knew that it was all just a dream, and she hoped that he did too, but she never discouraged it. It was good to have dreams even if they were only pipe dreams that may never come true. Instead of establishing a trapline hundreds of kilometres from the nearest town, Grandpa drove every day through the industrial areas of the city to the spot that they call Papaschase Industrial, where he tanned hides commercially.

Charlie and Grandpa didn't get along. Grandpa thought that Charlie was old enough to be supporting the family. Charlie thought that Grandpa was a hard-ass. They butted heads right from the moment that Charlie and Daniel walked through the door and came to live with them permanently. Granny figured that the two of them had the same personality. When she looked at Charlie she saw a younger version of Grandpa. Stubborn, hardened to the world, a man who belonged in the early eighteen hundreds hunting bison on the Prairies with the Métis. But the two of them were stuck in a city that didn't recognize Métis men and how they moved across the landscape, and the Métis men didn't recognize the authority of people who came in to boss them around on a land where their ancestors had hunted bison since time immemorial.

Charlie moved out when he was seventeen. He dropped out in his last year of high school and got a job working construction, building all the new high-rises downtown.

"Don't you get dizzy being so high up?" Granny had asked Charlie when he first got the job.

"I like pretending to be a pigeon," Charlie replied.

"I think you're more of a golden eagle," Granny said. "I'll keep my feet on the ground, thank you very much."

"Okay then," Charlie said.

Charlie had had his run-ins with the law. Nothing serious, just the odd bar brawl or fight on the Avenue and a stint in the Young Offender Centre. He had a couple assaults and public intoxication charges. Nothing that couldn't be overlooked for a job lifting shit and moving it into place on top of the city's skyscrapers. The incidents usually began when someone said something about Indians in one of the bars Charlie was drinking in. He didn't take that well. Charlie had been hearing it his whole life, and instead of replying with words, he did it with fists. He had a bit of a reputation on the Avenue for being a tough motherfucker. Not tough enough that the gangsters wanted to get him, but tough enough that you didn't mess with him if you knew better. That reputation had served Daniel well most of his life. Most people knew to steer clear of him or else Charlie would fuck them up. Most people.

Keesha was the first and only visitor who came to see Daniel at the hospital. The morphine haze had faded into a Percocet glow and he had spent the past few days drifting in and out of sleep and trying to remember YouTube music videos of songs he liked. Without a phone, the hospital was boring. Daniel had found himself reverting back to A Tribe Called Red's "Suplex" and the video that went with it. The old-school wrestlers in the video made him think about going to matches at the Alberta Avenue Community Centre back in his childhood, when the semi-pro wrestlers came through the city. Once a month, Granny would take him down there and pay the five-dollar admission to watch the Green Machine fight Dirty Irish. Those dudes were staples. But one time a wrestler named Big Bear was there, a big Cree dude with a long ponytail, and Daniel made sure they got there super early so they could get front-row seats for his match. Granny would usually bring in goose jerky and on the odd occasion the little Halloween chocolate bars she bought year-round when they had some excess cash. Big Bear's signature move was the Tomahawk Chop, which he smashed down on the head of whoever he was wrestling. Daniel couldn't remember his opponent's name. Big Bear had only ever come to the monthly wrestling match once. But that was the one that stuck out in Daniel's mind.

"Do you remember a wrestler named Big Bear?" Daniel asked Keesha.

"Sounds like cultural appropriation to me," Keesha replied.

"Nah, he was like this big fucking Cree dude. Had a move called the Tomahawk Chop."

"Yeah, that's definitely fucked. Some old racist running the show probably set that up for him or something. Was that on WWE?" Keesha said.

"Nah, over at the Avenue Community Centre," Daniel said.

"I never went to that," Keesha replied.

"You missed out," Daniel said. "Wrestling is the shit."

"Did they catch the kids who did this to you?" Keesha ran her fingers along the cast on Daniel's arm.

"Ah, who cares? Little fucks obviously needed the money more than I did."

"What money?" Keesha asked.

"The weed money." The Percocet made Daniel forget that he was supposed to hide from Keesha the fact that he sold weed. His words just seemed to pour out.

"You were selling weed?" Keesha asked.

"Well yeah. Don't you?"

"No."

"I ran into Charlie the other day. Your bro was fucking livid. He took it as an insult, you know."

"I can imagine."

"But then he was pissed because he couldn't smash down some kid. Wouldn't be right he said." Alex paused, put down the guitar, walked over to the fridge and opened the door. "Got any beers?" He asked. Daniel didn't respond. He grabbed a blanket from the back of the couch that Granny had made him as a high school graduation present. It had big bears all over it and little infinity symbols on the edging. For some reason, at that moment, Daniel remembered another blanket Granny had made him when he was a kid. That one had glow-in-the-dark stars woven onto it. Daniel had it during the few months he was in a group home before his Granny came and got him out of there. Daniel figured he must have been around ten years old at the time. Too old for the glowing stars to be enough of a comfort for him to fall asleep in that place.

Alex returned without any beer.

"So like I was saying. Charlie's fucking pissed, so he goes and scares the shit out of one of the kid's older brothers. Think his name's Kenny or something, I dunno. He scares the shit out of him and tells him that the money better be back to him right away. So I guess we'll see what happens."

"Yeah man, to be honest I don't really care," Daniel said. His head was feeling all sorts of fuzzy and he was finding it hard to register the words that Alex was saying.

"Your brother scares the shit out of me," Alex said.

"Can I borrow your phone? I should probably call Granny," Daniel said.

"Sure buddy." Alex tossed his phone over to Daniel. Daniel missed the catch and it smoked him in the chest.

"Ah fuck," he yelled in pain. Alex started laughing.

"Sorry dude, my bad." Alex kept laughing. "Fuck that's funny. Oh man, sorry, ha ha ha."

Daniel grimaced through it and dialled Granny's number. She picked up on the last ring before the answering machine.

"Hello?" Granny said.

"Granny, it's me. How're you doing?" Daniel said.

"I'm alright my boy. How are you feeling?" She asked.

"I've been worse, you know. Nothing that a couple days on the couch won't fix."

"How much money you lose?"

"Four hundy or so."

"That's a lot," Granny said.

"We'll make it back you know. These things happen." Daniel looked over at Alex. They made eye contact, Alex nodded and then looked down and started lightly strumming a G chord.

"Okay, come see me soon." Granny finished the conversation. That was one of the longest conversations Daniel had ever had on the phone with her. Granny wasn't one to talk on the phone. She never had been. She must be worried about him, Daniel figured.

"Want to steal your aunt's van and drive me up to the north side tomorrow?" Daniel asked Alex.

"I'll try. We might have to buy her a six-pack or something. But she knows you got beat up by a twelve-year-old so she might take pity on you," Alex said with a smirk on his face.

"Oh fuck off, he was sixteen at least," Daniel said. He laughed and then closed his eyes and stretched out on the couch.

"I'm gonna go grab some beer, man. I'll be back later." He heard Alex's voice trail off as he drifted into sleep. There were no glow-in-the-dark stars this time. Just the cold darkness of Percocet.

The next day, Alex showed up with his aunty's Dodge Grand Caravan. Daniel limped out of the house. Each step still sent pain through his ribs no matter how much pain medication he took.

"Come on old lady. Let's go," Alex called from the driver's side window. Daniel gave him the middle finger and shuffled across the street to the van. He got in. Alex reached over and handed him his old cellphone, the one that the kids had stolen when they mugged him.

"I ran into Charlie last night, dude. He had this for you. Told me that the kid's brother brought this back but he didn't have any of the money."

"Figured. Didn't think the kid would be putting it into his savings account or some shit like that," Daniel said. He looked down and the phone screen was all cracked and broken. He pressed the home button, and it loaded up. The screen background was a picture of his ex-girlfriend Ashley—he should really change that—but at least the phone worked.

Alex dropped Daniel off at Granny's apartment. He told Daniel he had to go run some errands. But Daniel knew that really meant heading down the road to the pub. What twenty-two-year-old runs errands? Daniel forgot that he couldn't hop over the balcony like he normally did. He caught Granny's eye through the window and she walked over to the side fire exit and opened up the door for him. Granny didn't say a word and Daniel hobbled behind her into the apartment.

"Hold up Granny, I can barely keep up with you," Daniel said as the two of them turned down the hall toward her apartment. Granny had a smirk on her face.

"Guess we should have a race then," she said.

They got into the apartment after what felt like walking the length of the south side up to the north side but in reality it was just a hallway. Daniel collapsed onto the couch, popped a Percocet and started massaging his ribs.

Granny went into the room where she grew and kept the weed. Daniel figured she'd be coming out with some, but instead she came back with a big piece of birchbark that had been stripped from a tree.

"Hold out your arm," Granny said. Daniel held out his broken arm. Granny grabbed some scissors and snipped down the cast.

"I don't know if you're supposed to take this off," Daniel said.

"I don't think you're supposed to be taking those pills like you are," Granny responded. She slipped the cast off and then placed the birchbark around his broken arm. She took the cast and punched little holes in each side of where the cut line ran down the length of it. After she had matching holes in each side, she ran a thread through them. She then put the cast back on Daniel's arm and used the thread to tie it tight around the birchbark that had been put in place.

"There, that should do it," Granny said, as she finished tying the last thread. "Is it tight enough?" She gave it a little shake.

"Owww," Daniel grimaced, pain shooting through his arm. Granny laughed and stopped shaking his arm.

"You'll be fine," she said. "Did you get a phone?"

"Charlie found my old one."

"Good."

"He was trying to get the money back too, but I think that's a lost cause."

"Yeah, it's not worth it," Granny said.

"I might not be able to head to the university for a few days. I feel like death right now," Daniel said.

"Maybe Alex could take some for us?" Granny said. She looked up at Daniel with her grey eyes on fire.

"I could ask, but I'd rather not get that many people in on it. Alex wouldn't be good at the U either. He'd get busted or kicked out in a second, looking and acting the way he does. Security would definitely be asking him for his student ID."

"Just give him your ID card," Granny said.

"I don't know if that's a good idea. Then I could get screwed when he gets busted," Daniel said.

"I thought you didn't care about getting kicked out of school," Granny said. "What's the worst thing that could happen? You go get a job with Charlie? That would probably be better for you anyways."

"I don't care about school."

Granny shrugged her shoulders and turned on the TV to the Blue Jays game.

"Stroman's pitching, should be a good one," Daniel said.

When the game finished Daniel hobbled up to the pub to find Alex sitting at a table for four, solo, with an almost empty pitcher of Canadian on the table and two glasses. Alex's eyes were fixed on a couple old dudes who were playing the VLTs. Daniel sat down at the table and poured himself a pint. He watched the golden liquid bubble up and softly foam, pop and then recede back into liquid. *I wonder how many people have written poems about beer*, Daniel thought. Without taking his eyes off the guys playing VLTs or acknowledging Daniel's presence in any way, Alex reached across the table, picked up his glass of beer and took a big swig.

"Those fucking guys have probably sunk a good grand each into those machines tonight," Alex's speech had a notable slur. "Wish I had a grand. I'd spend it better than that, you know."

"Fuck would you do with a grand?" Daniel asked.

"Nose beers, bud, nose beers," Alex said. "Nah, joking, I would probably go to Mexico or some shit."

"And then some Mexi-nose beers?" Daniel said. He laughed and took a swig from his pint now that the pour had settled. He hadn't had a sip of booze since his accident and the first sip now made him think of one of the first times he ever drank a beer. Probably back when he was ten or eleven years old, and they all seemed to have this unique carbonated taste that he couldn't get enough of, even back then.

"God that tastes good," Daniel said. "That's smooth, dangerously smooth." He took another sip. He hadn't been feeling like his chatty self since he got jumped. But these beers, these helped.

"You imagine sinking that much money into something so stupid?" Alex kept going. "I just can't figure it out. No one ever wins."

"Isn't that the truth, bud." Daniel took another big swig. Now he was feeling really chatty. "Lightweight," he muttered to himself. Then Daniel looked around the room hoping that the beautiful Cree server who was usually working was around. She was behind the bar pouring pints. Daniel tried to catch her eye but attempted to avoid directly staring. He couldn't figure it out, and she never looked over at him. He gave up and just hoped she would be coming by the table.

"Guy like that, we could hammer on him, grab his wallet and be out of here before anyone could say anything," Alex said.

"Fuck that, this is Granny's spot. They know me," Daniel said.

"They don't know me."

"You think I can run like this? Have fun man, but I'm going to say I don't know you for shit," Daniel said.

"Oh, chill. I'm just playing, didn't think you'd be so scared," Alex said.

"Just being realistic, man. Go steal a bike."

Last summer, Daniel and Alex had a good racket stealing bikes from the university and selling them back up on the Avenue. Daniel always enjoyed the rush of stealing bikes. He called it his summer job. While most of his classmates were off interning, bartending, travelling, moving back to their hometowns, Daniel was a semi-professional bike thief on the campus. Once the semester started up, though, he would stop stealing the bikes. That would just get messy. But Alex usually kept it going a bit longer on his own.

"You hungry? I see you got beer," the server said. Alex didn't acknowledge her at all, he was still intent on the VLT dudes. Daniel looked up at her. "Oh shit, it's you. You look terrible, what happened?" she asked. She was wearing a crisp white T-shirt. Daniel wasn't sure how she managed to keep it clean of hot sauce, especially since every night was wing night. Daniel could see a feather tattoo running down her arm—it looked fresh, the ink was real dark even on her brown skin.

"Ah, long story," Daniel answered. He hoped that he looked like a badass, a tough guy, and that she'd be impressed with his injuries.

"He got jumped," Alex said. His first sign that he even noticed the server was standing at the table.

"Oh no. You okay?" she asked.

"Yeah..."

"Well obviously, if you're here," she continued. "But your face, it's busted up."

"Tell me about it, got a nasty limp too. Just shuffling everywhere," Daniel said.

"Sorry, I didn't mean to say you looked rough," the server said. "But you do."

"Well thanks!" Daniel was starting to feel a bit more confident with the beers in his blood. "Granny gave me some good medicine so I'm doing okay."

"I bet she did. Her and her friend were in here the other day watching the afternoon Jays game and playing crib. She didn't mention you got hurt though."

"Nah, she wouldn't. I'm sorry, I don't know your name." Daniel held out his hand, prompted by the liquid courage.

"Cheryl. I don't know yours either."

"Daniel."

"Okay, I'm going to go get your pitcher filled up. Food?" Cheryl asked.

"Nah, we good," Alex answered.

Cheryl dropped the pitcher off and went about serving the other customers. Daniel sat there and watched the endless sports highlight reel playing on the TV above the bar. Alex kept staring as he had been all night. Daniel was used to that at this point, the guy was always fixated on something. Daniel kept looking at Cheryl, but tried to keep it from being creepy. He was starting to figure out an idea for how they could keep selling. Even while he was laid up.

"Think she'd sell weed for us? At least until I get back on my feet?" Daniel asked.

"No. She's too nice, man. Not that being a pot dealer is all that tough," Alex said.

"I think she might. She's our age, looks smart as fuck. Way smarter than us. I bet she'd fit right in on campus."

"What Native has ever fit in on campus?"

"She could pass for Asian maybe? I don't know."

"Why don't you just sell out of the apartment? Make those university bitches come to you?"

"'Cause then we're actually selling weed. Then that means actual fucking drug dealers might find out. That means we get the shit kicked out of us or worse. That's why. Fucking idiot," Daniel said. "Don't be dumb man. You want to go gang it up? Have fun. I'm going to just keep this thing riding."

"I'd be an awesome gangster," Alex said.

"You'd be a terrible gangster. Anyway, I'm going to ask her."

Daniel caught Cheryl's eye and she came walking over to the table.

"You boys need anything else?" she asked.

"Can I ask you something?" Daniel said.

"Sure." Cheryl pulled out one of the chairs and sat down beside them.

"You ever sell weed?" Daniel asked.

"Pfft." Cheryl started laughing. "I thought you were going to ask me out or something. Not ask me about weed. Ha." She stood up. "I know how the rest of this conversation goes, so I'm just going to tell you no right now."

"He's not a cop," Alex added.

"No shit," Cheryl said. She stood up and started walking away.

"Well, if I asked you out what would you have said?" Daniel called after her.

"I guess you'll just have to figure that out."

They were driving back to the Avenue later that night. Alex was toasted, but he was doing alright on the pedals and no one was out on the roads except the odd city bus. "You think Cheryl would want to hang out with me?" Daniel asked.

"I dunno man." Alex took the turn into the apartment parking lot a little too sharp and the van went over the curb. Pain shot through Daniel's leg as they bounced back onto the road.

"Watch where you're fucking going dude. Fuck that hurt," Daniel said.

If that little shit Daniel isn't going to school, I don't know how I'm going to make enough money for the Island, Granny thought. Her friends all laughed at her when she told them about her plans to get away from the north side. Granny dismissed their laughter and little comments about her plan. *None of them have ever done anything on their own,* Granny thought. *They'd just as soon sit here and die rather than try and do anything else.* Granny had never been one for sitting idle. She had always taken control of her own situation and this wasn't going to be any different. There was no use waiting for Daniel to figure out what he was going to do. That might take too long, and time wasn't exactly something that Granny had lots of. What she did have lots of, though, was weed. More and more of it was growing and ready for harvesting all the time, and none of it was moving anymore.

Granny met up with her friends at the cafeteria in the assisted living building. They dealt a hand of crib and started chatting. None of them had to think about the numbers or the cards anymore, they just played automatically, holding onto the cards that would lead to potential double straights, pairs and the odd fifteen here and there. Though they all knew that chasing fifteens was a beginner's game.

"Any of you ever try smoking marijuana?" Granny said. *No use beating around the bush,* she thought.

"Marijuana, that's illegal. Thirty-one for two," her friend Morene responded.

"Yeah, booze was illegal too and you used to chug that back," Granny said.

"I hear that Dr. Wallace is starting to prescribe it. A couple people in the building have prescriptions. Fifteen for two," another lady said.

"My neighbour is always smoking it. It reeks up the whole hallway," another added.

"I don't think I could smoke it. It would make me want to smoke cigarettes again. I had such a hard time quitting those. Fifteen two, four and a pair is six," Morene said.

"I heard you go insane if you smoke it. You'll want to jump out of a window or something. Two runs of three is six and a pair is eight."

"You missed a fifteen there, Gladys," Granny said. "I don't think it's going to make anyone jump out of a window."

"I'd probably try it if I could eat it. I watched a show on edibles," Irene said. "But there's no way I would smoke it."

"I'd probably try eating it too," another lady chimed in. "I wish that old bastard down the hall would eat it. Smells like a bunch of skunks mating in our area."

The next day Granny took a cab a couple blocks over to the Castle Downs common which had a grocery store, a McDonald's and a public library. First she went to the McDonald's and got herself a large coffee and two cheeseburgers. She ate those and then brought her coffee over to the library. Behind the desk, a couple ladies were working. One was significantly younger than the others. Granny made a point of going up and chatting with her specifically. She'd probably be able to help.

"Do you have any books on baking with marijuana?" Granny asked.

The young librarian looked startled.

"No ma'am. I really don't think we do," she sputtered.

"Are you sure?" Granny asked again.

"I'm sorry ma'am, no, we don't."

"Okay, whatever," Granny said. She turned and started walking toward the doors. She was about to open them when one of the older librarians who was at the desk caught up to her.

"Ma'am, sorry, were you looking for edible resources?"

"Yeah, sure," Granny responded.

"I think I can help you find some online stuff. I don't think we have any books but here, let's pull up a website on it."

"I ain't touching one of those computers," Granny said.

"No problem, I can help with it," The librarian sat down at one of the public computers. Granny pulled up a chair beside her.

"Alright, here we go." Within seconds the librarian pulled up a page full of recipes for butters, brownies, cookies, even a caramel sauce.

"Do you mind if I write these down?" Granny asked.

"I can print them for you if you wish, but it'll cost ten cents per page," the librarian said.

"No, I'll just write them down, thank you."

"Best of luck with your baking, bring some by for me to try if you want," the librarian said. She winked at Granny.

"Thank you very much," Granny said. She tried to hide her excitement from all the other people shuffling around the library and then on the sidewalks as she headed over to the Sobeys. But as she walked through the doors of the grocery store, she let out a big grin and had to do her best from letting out a whoop. She looked down and checked the recipes that she had written out and headed toward the baking supplies aisle. She didn't need Daniel for this. She didn't need anyone but herself.

As she baked her weed away, Granny thought back to OG kohkom. Granny had always felt sorry for her. Granny's parents and her little brothers and sisters were all forced off the road allowances in the sixties and had to make their way to Edmonton for work. Granny had been eighteen at the time and had been living in the city for the past few years in Strathcona, just a few blocks away from what had been the Papaschase Reserve where OG kohkom was born. Granny's father got a job working in the sewers; her mom tended to all the little kids. They brought OG kohkom with them. She wanted nothing to do with going back to the land where she was born. The family found a cheap house on the Avenue of Champions, and even though it was close, OG kohkom wouldn't go south of the river. Too much pain, too much blood and tears, she would tell Granny when Granny offered to take her down there in a cab. I'll just sit up here and die with all these kids crawling all over me. And that's exactly what she did.

Granny missed her all the time. She had known her better than she had known her parents. She missed the sounds of the Cree language, and the way that OG kohkom spoke it. She missed the parties that they used to go to when she was a kid. She missed her Uncle Jimmy who had lived with them on and off until he went through the ice on the Amisk River. His body turned up the next spring when the river broke up. She missed the little log and sod cabin that they had lived in and the cast iron pot of tea that never left the top of the wood-burning stove. She missed filling it up with spruce needles and dried wild mint.

"Granny wants us to come up and try her weed brownies," Daniel said to Alex. They were sitting around Daniel's apartment.

"What?"

"Yeah. Apparently last week Granny got a couple recipes somehow and she's been rocking those. She doesn't want to sample though."

"Don't smash from your own stash. Smart move, Granny," Alex said.

"What are you, some shitty nineties weed comedy?" Daniel said.

"I think the nineties were cool alright. Let's go see Granny," Alex said. He then stood up and went to grab his coat.

"Let's go up tomorrow. There's a Jays playoffs game against Texas I wouldn't mind catching. Might as well get high as shit for it."

"Oh fuck yeah, I'm going to destroy some Wii bowling, too." Alex threw his coat back down, walked into the kitchen and grabbed a couple beers from the fridge. "Love that Wii bowling. Did you ever ask out the pub lady?" He tossed Daniel a Pilsner.

"Cheryl, nah, she's like that unattainable hot, you know."

"She winked at you."

"Shit, I really don't know man. Maybe next time."

"What about Keesha?"

"Oh shit, we should call her. She'd love to go and eat Granny's weed brownies."

Keesha picked up Daniel and Alex from the Avenue of Champions in her half-ton Dodge Ram.

"Shit, this is that River Cree money, yo," Alex said when he hopped in the front seat. He had called shotgun and somehow that was still a thing that all of them just recognized automatically. Keesha had a bunch of bags of chips in the back seat of her truck. Daniel sat down beside the Doritos Zesty Taco bag and automatically opened it up.

"Save that for Granny's," Keesha yelled at him. Daniel responded by shoving his hand into the bag, taking out a handful and shoving it into his mouth. Chip crumbs went flying everywhere. "You fuck, don't eat all of those."

"Relax."

"I will beat the shit out of you if you don't leave some for Granny. You know she loves those chips."

"She'd want her favourite grandson to have some."

"No, she really wouldn't, she'd call you fat. Tubby."

Granny watched the three of them as they got out of the black truck and hopped hockey style over her balcony. *Good kids,* Granny thought.

"Granny!" Keesha yelled as she came through the door and wrapped Granny up in a big hug.

"Keesha, my girl. How's your aunty and kohkom?"

"They're good, Granny. They said to say hi and that you should come visit them sometime at the Elders' centre. They play cards there most days."

"namoya, maybe if this boy would drive me eh?" Granny pointed with her lips toward Daniel.

"Don't you think Daniel's getting fat?" Alex sat down on the couch and cracked a beer.

"I'm not getting fat," Daniel said.

"Nothing wrong with being a big boy," Granny said.

"I'm not fat!"

"Suuure," Keesha said. "Granny, you should come visit me at the River Cree then?"

"Ah pfft, you work too late in the day for me. I like the mornings on the bus. Breakfast specials, you know," Granny said. She stood up and walked toward the kitchen. Above the stove she had a couple old ice cream pails loaded up with brownies. She grabbed one of the ice cream boxes and walked back over to Keesha, Daniel and Alex, who were all sitting on the couches. Daniel had changed the channel from CBC to Sportsnet. The first pitch was about to be thrown. "Okay kids. The recipe said one brownie each."

"I think I'll start with half of one," Keesha said. "Just in case."

Daniel and Alex each took one from the pail. Keesha took one, broke it in half and put the other half back in.

"Okay, you kids have to let me know how they are. I don't think I want them too strong or the notokwesow moniyaw around here will throw a fit."

"Just strong enough to knock a bear out?" Keesha asked.

"namoya, more a sisip," Granny replied.

Two hours later the ball game was in the seventh inning. Alex was lying spread out on the floor staring at the ceiling. His eyes were closed but he was still cheering along with the Blue Jays' announcer's calls. Daniel was in Grandpa's old rocking chair. He had emptied the bag of Doritos into a bowl and was slowly eating each chip one at a time while he watched José Bautista come up to bat.

"You're going to need some sort of code, Granny," Daniel said, spraying chip crumbs everywhere as he spoke. "Like, I use that reference one at the university."

"You do not need that," Alex said.

"No, you do. You need to have people coming over and saying that they want to have tea, or play Yahtzee or some old person shit like that."

"Tea sounds good," Granny said.

"Didn't they call dope 'tea' back in the day?" Keesha asked. Granny and her were sitting at the kitchen table beading earrings.

"Beats me." Granny shrugged her shoulders. "Those are some crazy colours my girl."

Keesha held up an earring that had a circular pattern of orange, purple, pink and blue beads. "I wanted to capture a sunrise," she said.

"This one time I saw a beautiful sunrise," Alex called from the kitchen.

"Cool bro. Got anything else to add to that?" Keesha said.

"No," Alex said. He started giggling, stood up and walked over to grab the bowl of chips from Daniel.

"You ever feel like you're an animal or something?" Alex asked. "Sometimes I think I'm part coyote. I like cruising around alleys, getting into garbage and shit."

"Do coyotes care about sunrises?" Keesha asked.

"Probably not. They're into chips though," Alex shoved his head right into the bowl of Doritos and started chomping down.

"You idiot," Keesha said. "I wanted some of those."

"Daniel's a big old fat buffalo," Alex said, raising his head out of the bowl. "Big ol' bat fuffalo."

Keesha, Daniel and Alex all started giggling. That turned into howling, and they got caught up in the laughter, unable to stop.

Granny was feeling confident in her recipe. She had taken each of the brownies and divided them in two. She would sell them in a smaller portion than she had originally thought. According to Keesha—after they had all settled from the laughing fits—a small portion was enough to get the job done. The last thing Granny wanted was for one of the ladies in the building to think she had gone crazy or something like that. Granny was sure that she would get booted from the building if someone found out that she had been growing weed in her storage closet, or that she was now planning on selling it in baked-good form to the residents of the building and their friends. After Grandpa had died, the nurses and aides never really came into her room. Granny was as self-sufficient as you could be, and other residents required a lot more of the nurses' attention. She kept a pretty clean place, and even when the cleaners came in once a week, they just stuck to the main areas and the bathrooms. They didn't bother touching the storage closet. And as Daniel had told Granny back when they had first started growing, it's not like they'll be able to trace extra electricity usage back to your unit. They'll just think you have one of those snoring machines hooked up or something like that.

Granny wasn't sure what she would do if she got kicked out. Probably would have to go and move in with Daniel. She was sure that he would be fine kicking out his roommate; Granny had never even met her, and she usually met everyone Daniel hung around with. Charlie, on the other hand, was her mystery grandson. She knew Charlie lived a harder life than Daniel. That—that was Charlie's choice. She rarely talked to him, and never had the same relationship with him that she had with Daniel. Charlie had always found solace in the Avenue, and in his friends who had helped him survive that world. Daniel, though still connected to the community, had been able to branch out a bit. Granny would never ask to move in with Charlie, even though his apartment probably had more room than Daniel's.

Granny would have liked to see Charlie more though. She wouldn't tell anyone that, but his absence from her life pained her. She knew that Charlie always had Daniel's back and would support her in anything. But he was just the kind of guy who didn't have much use for visiting an old lady up on the north side. He was more intent on survival. Always had been.

Granny started spreading the word about the weed brownies at the morning workout class. The assisted living building brought in instructors daily to run the attendees through different stretches and movements. Granny went down more for the coffee and cards afterwards than for the workout itself. She considered the coffee and cards her reward for doing something physical.

Turned out more people in the building were interested in the healing properties of weed than she ever thought would be. Word travelled fast, as she figured it would. The building was rife with gossip most of the time. This was just the latest. Within a couple days she could barely keep up with the demand for the brownies. There was a continuous line of old people strolling down the halls with their walkers and wheelchairs toward her apartment for tea.

"I'll take two please," an old man requested. He came into her apartment and sat down at the sewing table that Granny had transformed into a makeshift desk. She had placed it in the front entrance of her apartment to block nosy seniors from coming in and wandering around. This way she just kept them in the entryway. One at a time. The way she liked.

"Two what?" Granny said.

The old man leaned in close and tried his best to whisper, "Two of those marijuana brownies. Boy do they make puzzling more fun."

"Forty bucks please."

"Forty bucks? That's a bottle of whisky," the old man said.

"Take it or leave it."

"Well, what if I told the building on you."

"awas, you're going to tell the nurses that I'm selling weed brownies? They're going to think you've got dementia and lock you up in full care."

"I was just joking." The old man gave Granny the money.

Granny became so busy she didn't have time to go out to the River Cree with Morene anymore. Granny suspected that the staff knew what was happening. But because people were more docile when they were all stoned up, the staff let it go on; it made their jobs easier. The weed moved fast and the old coffee can that Granny kept in the back of her fridge started filling up with more money than she had ever seen before. Way more than Daniel had been bringing her. Once the first coffee can had a couple grand in it, she moved it out and put it in the freezer behind the frozen leftover spaghetti noodles. Then she started filling up another can.

Soon she was getting invited to other assisted living and seniors' buildings' bake sales. She began touring around the north side; her friends kept her in the loop when another bake sale was happening. Granny often had to pay an entry fee to support the seniors' recreation program or something, but after that it was straight cash. And a lot of those people she sold to ended up coming back to her building to buy straight from her. They even took cabs over to see her. It got to the point where Granny had her oven running twenty-four hours a day. Then she started using her friends' ovens during the day to keep up with the demand.

* * *

The headlines were everywhere. LIBERALS COMMIT TO LEGAL-IZING MARIJUANA IF ELECTED. TRUDEAU TO LEGALIZE DOPE. MARIJUANA LEGALIZATION IN NEAR FUTURE? You couldn't go anywhere without people talking about it or referencing it. The Liberals had added it to their platform for the upcoming federal election. On campus, Daniel was flipping through an issue of the university newspaper and reading articles on it.

"I didn't think they would actually do it. Or commit to it," Daniel said. Keesha sat across the table from him. She was reading an Indigenous studies textbook and highlighting passages.

"They still need to get elected," Keesha said.

"What happens if they do? I'm going to be out of a job."

"I'm sure it will still be a while before they figure it all out. And then a rollout plan. These things take time. Government doesn't work fast."

"I dunno. What about Granny too? She started running out of bud even. I had to pick up a pound from one of Charlie's buddies the other day so I could keep her in her baking supplies."

"I don't think they'll get elected."

"You also said the NDP wouldn't get elected in Alberta," Daniel said.

"I was wrong."

"Goddamn government putting my granny out of a job." Daniel leaned back in his chair. He didn't sell nearly as much weed as he used to now that Granny was cranking out her baking for the building. He didn't need to. Just enough to cover the cost of the bags of dope that he had to buy now that Granny had used up all the bud she had grown. She had a few more plants coming along but they wouldn't be ready for harvest for a month at least. There were a couple people on campus that he still helped out. But he didn't take any new clients, or old clients that he didn't like. It was strictly friends at this point. That was enough for him. Ever since he had gotten smashed up, he was a bit hesitant to carry larger sums of cash on him. Or that much dope. It was just a matter of time until another kid tried to roll him. Daniel's wounds had healed up fine. He still had a bit of bruising on his arm from when he ditched the cast, but besides that it was all good. The only thing that remained was that he really just didn't want to get jumped again.

"You think I should try and bead Cheryl a pair of earrings? She'd date me then, eh?" Daniel asked.

"First, you don't know how to bead," Keesha said. "Her cousin is a big-time powwow dancer and I'm pretty sure I saw Cheryl out there too at the Ben Calf Robe powwow last year."

"I think I should be a powwow emcee." Daniel dropped into a deep rolling voice. "Redbullllllllllllll, take it away-eeeee."

"You're too Métis for that. Go emcee a jig-off or whatever it is you do. If that was Cheryl I saw, she had some tight regalia going on. Fancy too, and she almost hit the roof when she was dancing," Keesha said.

"I'd like to see that."

"She wouldn't date a chump like you. She'd be looking for an okichitaw like I am," Keesha said.

"Alex thinks you and I should date."

"I don't snag chumps, I just told you that. Especially chumps that distract me while I'm trying to study."

"Keener," Daniel said.

"Did you hear when the fucking professor told us that the Creator has a plan for us all?" Keesha asked. "He probably picked up that shit at one of those sweats white people pay hundreds of dollars to go to."

"Huh?" Daniel responded. "Sorry, I didn't hear you." He couldn't get Cheryl out of his head. He kept playing their last conversation over and over. Maybe that had been the opportunity to ask her to hang out and he blew it. What if she quit working at the pub? Would he ever be able to find her again? It was starting to get to the point where most of his days were occupied by endlessly wondering what she was doing. It was hard to speculate because he didn't know anything about her except that her hair mesmerized him, she worked at the pub and she could keep her shirts really clean. Studying was useless at this point. He had been sitting here with Keesha for what felt like hours and hadn't read past the first page of the chapter.

"I'm out. I'll catch you in class tomorrow," Daniel said.

"Where are you going?" Keesha asked.

"I gotta go ask her out," Daniel said. "Granny's probably due for some more weed by now, so I'll bring some up, then go and see what happens."

"How do you know she'll be working?" Keesha asked.

"The Creator has a plan for us all," Daniel responded. He waved his hand in a clockwise circle.

He wasn't going to have any beer or joints beforehand. Just straight up walk in there and ask her if she wanted to hang out, and then he'd leave. He wouldn't hang around and make things weird. It would look like a movie scene. There he would be, strolling in, wearing the black hoodie and jeans that had the fewest rips, and his Edmonton Oilers hat. She'd be standing behind the bar pouring a pitcher. He'd sit down right at the bar, she'd smile at him, say she'd be right back and then she'd go drop off the pitcher of beer. Daniel would take his hat off. When she came back, she'd ask him what she could get him and where his Granny was. Daniel would say that he didn't have time for a beer today, you know, to keep the mystery alive, even though there was nothing he had more of than time. Then he'd ask her if she wanted to go and watch the sunset at the End of the World. She'd ask where that was and he'd say it was just a ways from the university, and they could meet there for a coffee, then walk over. She'd say sure and that would be that.

And it almost went that way, word for word. Except that Daniel stumbled and stuttered his words when he asked her out, and there were guys sitting at the bar so he had to sit at a table. Also, Granny had insisted on coming with him because she needed a break from all the baking and sales.

"What do you think?" Cheryl asked Granny.

"You should probably say yes. Some of my friends have had their eye on him so he might not be available for long."

"Are these ladies I should be worried about?" Cheryl said.

"Not really, they're more into guys with cars and driver's licences. That's a hot thing in the assisted living building."

"I have a driver's licence," Daniel said.

"Yeah but you don't have a car, so what good is that?" Granny said. "My friends need cars too, you know. They don't want to ride the bus."

"Well, I have a driver's licence and a car, so I can pick you up," Cheryl said. She grabbed Daniel's phone from the table.

"What's your password?"

"Uh..."

"I need to add my contact."

"Um. Six, nine, six, nine."

Cheryl and Granny both stared at him.

"Real mature," Cheryl said.

The next Friday, Cheryl picked up Daniel and they drove down to the End of the World to watch the sunset. The End of the World was an abandoned support area for an old bridge that crossed the North Saskatchewan River and went up to the west side. Everything was long gone except an old concrete platform jutting out of the riverbank. It made a great viewpoint for watching sunsets. And as soon as the lighting got to a certain point, it would look like the platform dropped off into eternity. There were usually a couple groups of kids smoking weed and drinking at the spot, but they tended to keep to themselves. Daniel brought a six-pack of beer in his backpack. Once he and Cheryl sat down, he reached in and offered her one.

"No thanks. I don't drink," Cheryl said.

"Really? You work in a pub," Daniel said.

"Don't matter, I don't drink. Never really have."

"Why not?"

"Just not that into it. Too many people I know get sucked up in it and my kohkom told me you're not supposed to dance if you're drinking," Cheryl said.

"Makes sense." Daniel put the beer back in his bag. "Sorry."

"I don't care. Just not my thing. I'm not into drunks."

"Do you smoke weed?"

"Every once in a while. But I'm more into edibles than anything. I don't really like the way smoke feels in my lungs," Cheryl responded.

"Oh, Granny will like that," Daniel said. Then he laughed. "She's the edible queen."

"Granny? Like the one I serve in the pub all the time?"

"Yeah, she keeps that whole building supplied."

"That's funny, I've heard other seniors from the building mention that they were getting into weed brownies. I didn't know it was your granny though."

"Yeah, she's had it going on for a couple months now."

"So Granny's a dope dealer. Technically?" Cheryl asked.

"I guess so. But just as much as I'm a dealer. So not really."

"What do you mean?"

"I mean she just sells to people in her building to make money. I just sell to my friends to make enough to pay for her baking supply."

"That's dealing."

"But is it? I mean it's going to be legal I think."

"I'm not into hanging out if you're dealing. Too much shit comes with that."

"Fuck it then, I'm done," Daniel said.

"Really?"

"Only if we can hang out again."

"Pass," Cheryl said. She laughed and put her hand on Daniel's. He moved closer to her so their legs were touching as they hung over the ledge.

"Okay, if I tell you a joke and you laugh then can we hang out again?" Daniel asked.

"Maybe."

"Why do us Natives hate snow?" Daniel asked.

"Because it's white and on our land," Cheryl said.

"What, you heard that one before?"

"My mushum told me that one."

"Oh," Daniel said.

"But we can hang out still."

Daniel wasn't sure how he was going to break the news to Granny that he was going to stop selling weed. His heart hadn't ever really been in it. Since he got jumped, he had been really apprehensive about it all. He didn't really feel like getting the shit kicked out of him. It was just a matter of time until it happened again. He didn't want that. The only thing he wanted was

Cheryl. He still couldn't believe that they were hanging out. Most of the time he hopped on the bus up to the north side and they went for walks around the man-made lake and watched the birds. The lake was close to the pub and Cheryl could head over there before starting her shift. She told Daniel that she lived in a tiny two-bedroom apartment with her sister, her sister's four young kids and when he was back from his camp job up north, her sister's boyfriend. There was no room for Daniel over there. After her shift at the pub ended, Cheryl would drive over to his place, often arriving after two a.m. Daniel would skip school the next day and they'd lay around naked in bed, having sex over and over again, reading to each other, eating whatever food they could scrounge up. Daniel would pretend he knew how to play the guitar, and Cheryl would pretend he sounded good and encouraged him to start writing songs. They'd spend the entire day in bed until she had to leave for her next shift.

He had never met anyone with her dedication and passion for life. All she seemed to do was think of others. She told Daniel that she was saving money to go to community college and get a social work diploma so she could help First Nations kids. She delivered food to all her aunties and uncles on a regular basis. She went to ceremony with her family back in Saddle Lake regularly. She would take her nieces and nephews to the round dances. Keesha had told Daniel that he was going to have to shape the fuck up if he wanted to keep her around. Daniel had begged Keesha to help him with his essay writing for the class so that he might be able to drag his grades up enough to pass.

"Only if you're respectful to Cheryl," Keesha said. "If you're not I'm going to kick the shit out of you and then bring my brothers to kick the shit out of you and then we won't be friends anymore."

"Believe me, I'm good. I'm all in," Daniel had responded. He wanted to make sure that he and Cheryl kept going. But he was starting to worry that Granny needed his help.

Granny began to see less and less of Daniel as he started hanging out with Cheryl more. At the very start it was good, she would see him daily. Daniel would catch a ride up to the north side with Cheryl from his place. He'd usually stop in and see Granny first, even if just for a few minutes. But now Cheryl had told Daniel that he shouldn't be coming by so much because she didn't make as many tips when he was there. As much as Granny liked that Daniel was hanging out with a nice girl, she also missed the time she spent with her boy. *It's time to get out of here*, Granny figured. *My boy is growing up and moving on. I should too.* The last few months had been good for Granny financially. Her coffee can collection had been expanding to the point where she'd had to start stacking them in her quilting closet. She hadn't made a quilt since she started baking. *Once I get out to the island, I'll get back into quilting, I'll have time then*, Granny thought. *I'll make Cheryl a nice quilt for tuning up my boy.*

Daniel's baking supply drop-offs had become more and more inconsistent. Granny couldn't have that if she was going to stay on top of her baking orders. Business had become steady. The novelty of the weed brownies had worn off for the assisted living building and now it was just a select few she was selling to. She knew that a few of them bought extra so they could give them to their other friends and family. One of Granny's friends in the building had even said that one time her son, a cop, had been up to visit her and she had accidentally given him one of the weed brownies rather than the regular ones she had baked. Apparently her son the cop thought he got food poisoning and left the building veering all over the place. "He's a lightweight," the friend had commented.

But even with the weed-baking business levelling off, she still needed the money, especially now that she had decided it was really time to leave. Winter had come on strong, too. Baseball had ended, the Jays had lost in the division championship, and her body didn't like the cold weather. Vancouver Island was sounding nicer and nicer all the time. Some days, she wandered over to the library and had the librarians help her look up books on the Island. One of the librarians had even helped her look at a website of apartment listings. It was the same librarian who had helped her find the recipes. Granny made sure to bring her a couple brownies for her trouble.

Sometimes Granny thought about what would happen if the building staff busted her. She was pretty sure they wouldn't call the cops, but then again they might. If one of her regular customers, one of the paranoid ones, got in some sort of trouble, it might come back to her. So far she assumed that if there were any problems, the nurses had just treated them as the ramblings of senile old people. They would hopefully attribute it to all the stories on the news these days about the legalization of marijuana. That was probably what was triggering the ramblings. At least that's what Granny hoped they were thinking. If the cops came and she was going to be sent to jail, she'd just go and jump off the High Level Bridge like her brother had so many years before. Except she'd ask the eagles not to catch her on the way down. To Granny it was worth the risk to go and try something new. And hell, she had lived a good life already.

Granny called Charlie. A few days later, he showed up at her place with a bucket of KFC.

Granny put the chicken, fries, gravy and puke-green cole-slaw on two plates. She passed one of the plates to Charlie.

"How's work going?"

"It's fucking cold. What's up?" he said. Charlie wasn't much for small talk.

"I need a lot of weed."

"Pfft. Really? How many brownies are you making?"

"I'm going to make one last haul. I'll sell all of those and then I'm out."

"So, what, like an ounce?" Charlie asked. Granny laughed. He really had no idea of the extent of the operation that she had created in her building.

"Like four or five pounds."

"Bullshit. You're going senile, old lady. Do you know how much that is?" Charlie somehow managed to shove a whole chicken-leg bone in his mouth and dragged it down his teeth to get all the cartilage and meat off it. "A pound is like a fucking big-ass black garbage bag full."

"Really? Oh wow," Granny said. She stood up and walked into the kitchen and grabbed her wooden spoon out of the drawer. She came back and smacked Charlie on the head with it as hard as she could.

"What the fuck?" He coughed. "I almost choked on the salad."

"Don't call me senile you little shit. I'll whoop your ass."

"Fine, fine, fine. Well, get Daniel to get it for you."

"He's unreliable these days. He's in love."

"I know. I don't see him anymore," Charlie said.

"He isn't stopping by. That's one of the reasons I called you," Granny said. "You should call him too sometime."

"Nah, I'm too busy."

"So can you help me out?"

"I'll see what I can do." Charlie grabbed another piece of chicken and started sucking the meat off the bone. "So you're really going out to the Island eh? Grandpa hated the Island."

"Grandpa hated anywhere that wasn't home."

"What are you going to do out there?"

"Quilt, play cards, be warm," Granny said.

"Cool," Charlie said. They finished the chicken and Charlie left into the night.

God, he walks, acts and eats like a bear, Granny thought.

A couple days later she got a phone call from Charlie: "Leave the money in something on your coffee table. My buddy will drop it off around lunchtime today." Granny took the money out of her coffee can. She transferred it into one of the ice cream pails that usually held brownies. Then she set it on the table.

She was watching TV when an old minivan pulled up out front. It was a green Dodge Grand Caravan similar to the one

Grandpa had when the boys were young, and the one Alex often drove Daniel up to the north side with. *Why does everyone drive a minivan?* she thought. A white guy got out, walked to the back, opened the sliding door and just like Charlie said, dragged out a couple garbage bags. He walked over to the fence and threw them over. Then he hopped over and opened up the door. The guy just nodded at Granny in her chair. He didn't say a word, just left the bags in the middle of the living room floor, grabbed the ice cream pail from the table and left. Granny moved the bags into the storage closet. She called Morene to come down and help her. Then she got to work.

* * *

"I don't know how I'm going to tell her," Daniel said. He was sitting in his apartment with Cheryl and Alex.

"Shit, she's probably already stacked up," Alex said.

"She'll be fine," Cheryl said. "It's not so bad staying here."

"I think it's really the memory of my grandpa on this land here. She'd never tell you that, but his blood went back into the land when he died and she holds that close to her heart."

"I could just keep supplying her," Alex said.

"Do you really want to do that?" Cheryl asked. Since they had all started hanging out more, Cheryl and Keesha had been working on Alex to apply to nursing school. "You get arrested and your school applications might be fucked."

"Pfft I ain't worried about that," Alex said. He started soloing on the guitar, a hardcore riff that he had picked up at some point. Cheryl rolled her eyes.

"You're such a poseur. We all know you're not really gangster. Neither of you are," she said. "You're both softies who better figure their shit out."

"I'm going to go tell her," Daniel said. "I really hope this doesn't fuck everything up. I don't want to break her heart. She's really set on the Island."

"Want me to come with you? We can head up early before my shift."

"Nah, I better just go alone for this. You don't need to see Granny whipping me with her wooden spoon."

"Do you think she's going to be mad at me?" Cheryl asked.

"Shit no. If there's one thing Granny was always stoked on, it was when we quit something. She might be pissed though if I tell her that I want to do better in university. Or that I don't really want to get beat up again. She's never told Charlie or me once how to live our lives."

"Okay," Cheryl said.

"Besides, she likes you. You serve her and her crew beers," Daniel said. "I guess I'm really just worried that she's not going to be able to make enough to get out to the Island."

"I want her to like me," Cheryl said. Her eyes started welling up. "I know how much you mean to each other. I don't want her to resent me for asking you to stop selling dope."

"And that's why I can't supply weed to you anymore." Daniel finished talking. He had just poured it all out for Granny. How he was scared. How he wanted to build something with Cheryl. How he wanted to do better in school.

"I know. I'm good. Don't you worry about me," Granny responded.

"Are you sure? I know you had your heart set on the Island. We can still try and figure something out. I can apply for a bunch of scholarships or something and give you the money. Or I can get a job in the kitchen at the pub or something. I don't mind, really," Daniel said.

"Nah I'm good. Here, come see this," Granny brought Daniel over to the storage closet. She opened it up. The shelves were stacked with four-litre ice cream pails full of individually wrapped weed brownies.

"If you really want to help me, you can go pick me up one of those little freezers so I can get all these in there," Granny said. Daniel started laughing.

"Where the hell did you get the weed to make all of these?" he asked. "You're not giving your customers fake weed brownies are you?"

"Don't worry about it," Granny said. "Now go borrow your friend Keesha's truck and get me a freezer. I've already filled up Morene's and another lady's and I need to get these in there. Here you go." She gave Daniel four hundred dollars in twenties.

"She what?" Keesha asked, her voice coming in loud even though she had Daniel on the Bluetooth speaker in her truck.

"She has like fucking tons of weed brownies in there. I don't know how she made so many, and she wouldn't tell me either. There are so many ice cream pails full, it's ridiculous."

"So, you need me to come pick you up so we can go get Granny a little upright freezer?"

"Yes, please."

"Fuck yeah, but only because I want to see what Granny's got going on here. What a badass bitch," Keesha said.

"Are you kidding me?" Alex said.

"No, straight up. She has, like, tons. It's unbelievable. I don't know how she did it," Daniel said.

"Fuck yeah. What a gangster."

"Keesha and I just dropped off a freezer for her and loaded it up. We're going to bring her over to the pub if you want to join."

"Have a beer with the biggest gangster on the north side? What an honour. Shit yeah, I'm in."

"Can one of you help me find a place on the Island? I think you can do it on the internet. Then, as soon as I sell all of these brownies, I can get out."

"Cheers to that, Granny." Keesha, Alex, Daniel and Granny all raised their glasses and clinked them together. Cheryl raised an imaginary cup from behind the bar and pretended to clink it with them. "I can help you with that, no problem," Keesha said.

"Apparently there's usually a waiting list, so we should do it soon."

"I'm already on it," Keesha pulled out her phone and started Googling away.

"Get her a place with a hot tub and a pool. So when we come to visit we can get our lounge on," Alex said.

"Hell yeah," Daniel said.

"I think I'm going to get back into moonshining when I'm on the Island. All those fresh blackberries would make a great blackberry bounce," Granny said.

"I forgot about bounce. It's been all about the weed for so long now," Daniel said.

"Bounce'll make you go blind," Alex said.

"We'll miss you, Granny," Keesha said.

Granny smiled and sipped her beer. Never in her wildest dreams had she thought she would be able to make it out to the Island and now, now it was all within reach. Daniel and Alex were going to clear out the rest of the weed-growing equipment and the plants that were left. Then there would be no evidence in her place that there had ever been a grow op and ongoing weed bake sale happening. Only all the coffee cans filled up with twenties would be left. They should last for a while. Thirteen more years at least. The army pension could cover her rent, and the cash could cover food and groceries, card games and the casino. Her late husband would have had a heart attack if he knew how she and Daniel had made enough to get her out there. But that was alright because he was dead. She was alive and she was going to keep on living, and living well.

Two months later Granny gave away everything except for what she could fit in two suitcases and with a one-way ticket, boarded a direct flight from Edmonton to Comox, British Columbia.

5. MOVING ON

When I stopped selling weed, I ran out of money. Sounds pretty logical, but it fucked with my head for a bit. I had always had enough cash in my pocket for some food or some beers and darts. But now, shit, I'm flat broke. Like I better walk my sorry ass over to the Money Mart and stare at the *$10,000 for $20* sign. I can't imagine what I would do with ten thousand bucks. I'd buy myself and Cheryl some big-ass fancy steaks and a couple beers or wine, I think red wine—the kind that doesn't come in a box—is what you're supposed to have with fancy-ass steaks. There's a Moxie's over at the mall off the Avenue of Champions that we could hit up for those. I'm getting sick of scrounging up change for McDonald's Value Picks. Don't get me wrong, I love a good Junior Chicken. But when that's all a guy can afford, he's bound to start thinking about money.

Cheryl has been telling me I should get a job. Something to keep me out of trouble. I think she's scared that I'm going to start stealing bikes with Alex again. Which, don't get me wrong, has crossed my mind. At least when we do that I get to chill with my buddy all day long and have some adventures along the way.

"Who would hire me?" I asked Cheryl. We were chilling in my apartment. "Not exactly like I have a stellar resumé or anything like that."

"Lots of people applying for jobs don't have any experience. You could get something. Nothing wrong with serving or working at the mall or something," Cheryl said. She had the kind of personality that entailed showing up ten minutes before her shift and being the last to leave after making sure absolutely all her tasks were done. Glowing references from everyone. All the shit jobs I'd had, well, I didn't think I'd be able to put any of them on my resumé.

* * *

First job I had—not including the little-kid kind of shit, like setting tables up at the farmers' market—was at the neighbourhood grocery store. There wasn't much of an interview. I walked into the deli all ready to answer questions about meat, I guess, but the supervisor just shrugged her shoulders and asked when I could start and what days I could work. I told her I was available pretty much all the time. I wasn't into sports and the high school I went to didn't have much in the way of extracurricular activities.

"The standard wage is $7.50 an hour," the supervisor said. "There's no negotiation, so don't even try."

"Sounds great to me." I couldn't even imagine how rich I was going to be with $7.50 an hour. That was more money than I had ever dreamed I would have.

"It's twenty-five cents more than the bag boys make, so consider yourself lucky," the supervisor said. Her voice sounded like a million cigarettes. She stood up, ending the interview, and sure enough headed out toward the smoke pit behind the store. "You start tomorrow. Be here at four p.m.," she called, not bothering to turn around.

I was expecting a bit more ceremony around it all. A handshake, a form to sign, something like that. Then two days in, the supervisor up and quit. I figured she was already on her way out and couldn't really give a shit who she hired. The other deli employee, the supervisor's daughter, also quit on the same day. Turned out the deli and the rest of the grocery store worked on a seniority system. Whoever had worked there the longest got promoted. Two days into my job at the deli, I was made the supervisor. First up, I had to hire a couple part-time employees. Then I'd have to figure out how to spend the fifty-cent wage bump I got. eight dollars an hour. At this rate, I was going to get a pair of True Religion jeans in no time.

I called my friend Alex.

"Yo man, it's Daniel. You want a job?"

"Hell yeah."

"Cool, come by the grocery store," I said.

"What, a job at the grocery store?"

"Yeah buddy. In the deli, $7.50 an hour."

"Ah hell, why not."

Alex rolled over to the deli. We figured out the paperwork and found a couple white aprons in the back storage area. Then we started figuring out how to identify and slice the meat. I knew bologna but that was about it. Alex lived with his aunt and uncle and they often bought turkey, ham and other fancy shit, so he had a pretty good idea of what the deli was all about. Most of the time, we just poked the gross-ass headcheese and other weird-looking things that we'd find in the back. I had a pair of speakers that Granny had given me for my sixteenth birthday. I set those up and we'd blast Alexisonfire, Pennywise, Less Than Jake and Rancid. You could only hear it from the floor if you were in just the right position at the deli counter. Which happened pretty rarely, since most people didn't bother coming into the store, preferring the Safeway down the road.

"Check this out," Alex said. He had a big chunk of cooked ham in his hand.

"What?"

Alex walked over to the meat slicer. He set the blade so the slices would be as thin as you could get. Then he ran the cooked ham through it. The gelatinous blob started spraying ham everywhere.

"Let me try," I said.

"Fuck that."

"I'm your boss. Let me try."

"You ain't boss of shit," Alex said. Then he laughed and stepped back from the slicer. I hopped up on it and started spraying ham.

"Here, try and hit me," Alex said. He stood in front of the counter, right where a customer would stand. I started running the ham through faster, spraying a fountain of pink and white chunks into the air toward Alex. It was so close to going over the edge of the counter. So close. Then I ran out of cooked ham.

"Come on!" Alex yelled.

"Ah fuck it," I said. I walked over to the bakery and grabbed a big loaf of bread. Then I threw it over the aisles. I heard something crash when it landed.

"Oh shit," Alex said. We both scurried into the back storage area. A couple minutes later the store manager showed up.

"You didn't happen to see anyone throwing bread, did you?" she asked. I honestly couldn't tell her apart from the supervisor who had hired me. They were both probably in their forties, but living hard had put them on the wrong side of fifty.

"No ma'am."

"What's with the mess everywhere? You little shits better clean this up right away." She was pissed. She went and stood in the spot where the ham had been shooting toward the counter. "What the hell happened here?" she asked.

"Beats me," I said. I grabbed a couple rags and a mop. I looked over and Alex was taking a log of cooked ham out of the deli display case.

"What, is this cooked ham?" she yelled. "Why the hell is there cooked ham everywhere?" From behind me I could hear Alex turn the meat slicer on. A rainbow wave of cooked ham started spraying everywhere. Alex moved it faster than I did. He made it rain ham. And it rained ham all over the store manager. She was drenched in the weirdly wet, gelatinous, cold pink. She just stood there and stared at us in shock.

"Shit, let's go," I yelled. I ran into the back, grabbed the speakers and my backpack and took off running out of the store. Alex was right behind me. We ran down the Avenue until we got to his aunty's block. We were both still wearing our aprons.

"Think we'll get paid?" Alex asked.

A couple months later, I was walking down the Avenue of Champions and saw a *Now Hiring* sign outside the Mohawk. I rolled in and they hired me to pump gas on the spot. Ten dollars an hour, too. Making bank. Being a gas jockey was slick. I spent most of my time sitting in a shed behind the convenience store with this old grizzled dude who had been working there for twenty-five years. The old boy's pores just sweated diesel fumes and his breath always carried a bit of the whisky he was nipping on. He had this scam going on where he would "accidentally" damage a carton of cigarettes and then take them. Because you know, you can't have damaged smokes on the shelf. He would dump water on them. He would step on them. He'd conveniently lose them. And all the damaged, discarded cartons ended up in the shed. The only time he didn't have a smoke in his mouth was when the lady who worked inside the store would ring the bell for one of us to go and fill up some vehicle. He'd set his smoke down and wander around to the front. Sometimes, he would forget to set his smoke down and you'd hear the person whose car he was filling up start screaming as they watched him pouring Regular 87 with a lit dart hanging ash out the side of his mouth.

We'd alternate filling up the vehicles. When the bell rang, he'd roll out. Next car, I'd roll out. The Mohawk never got busy enough to warrant both of us being out there at the same time. It looked dank as fuck so most people commuting through avoided it. Most of the business came from Scratch 'N Win tickets, cigarettes and coffee.

The boss was this old rich white dude who drove around in a black Escalade. He was too cheap to hire someone to run his store for him. Every two weeks, he would show up to do payroll, scheduling and ordering. That was the only day that my shed buddy wouldn't be nipping on his whisky. Instead, he was out helping sweep up, changing garbages, filling up the squeegee tanks. All the stuff that we wouldn't do for two weeks at a time. I hated that day. It was a lot more fun hanging out in the shed and hearing my buddy's conspiracy theories than it was working.

"You know why this country has gone to shit?" he'd ask. I wouldn't respond because he was going to tell me whether I said anything or not. "It's because we're all part of one world order."

"They're all lizard people at the top."

"You ever been around the world? Well, I went up in a plane once and it looked flat to me."

"You know, 9/11 was an inside job."

I loved listening to his stories. I recognized the ridiculousness of them, but the passion he had for telling them and trying to convince me—not that I was arguing—made the listening worthwhile. It also really helped make an eight-hour shift fly by.

The Mohawk job went on for a few months. Then one day we're sitting in the shed smoking darts and the guy's going on about something when the door creaks open. There's the old rich white dude staring us down from behind his white sunglasses.

"What the hell are you two doing? Get up, you lazy pieces of shit," he said, spitting all over us. "I don't pay you two to fuck dogs in the back. What are you, homos or something?"

"Sorry, boss," the old grizzled dude mumbled. He walked past the boss and disappeared around the front.

"And you, you've been drinking, haven't you?" the boss said to me, more a statement than a question.

"No, sir."

"Then what's with the empty bottle back there. You think I'm some sort of fucking idiot?"

"That's not mine."

"Well it's sure as shit not Bill's, guy's been off the sauce for years," the boss said. He kicked the empty plastic mickey toward me. "So whose is it?" he asked.

I'd had enough of his shit at this point. "You know what? Fuck off, you tiny-cock fucknut."

"What?" he stammered.

"You heard me," I pushed him out of the way and ran past him.

"I bet you're the one been stealing cigarettes too," he yelled at my back. "Don't you ever fucking come back here."

So that was Mohawk. Not long after, I got accepted into university. All I wanted to do was work at a bookstore. I figured that was the kind of thing a university student would do. I had this image in my head of myself wandering through rows of book-shelves, talking literature and poetry with women who wore dark-rimmed glasses and had long black hair. That's what I figured other university students would look like. I'm sure I picked up that image from reading Jack Kerouac books. Because, really, I didn't have any clue what university was going to be like. But I did know I needed to make some cash to pay for school.

I hit up every Chapters and used bookstore in the city within biking or LRT distance. I filled out Chapters applications and dropped off resumés. It took me a couple days to get around the city to each one. I was confident that one of these massive bookstores would be hiring. Shit, I would have taken any job, I just really wanted one at a bookstore. If I got a job there, it would validate my image of myself as a university student. University students worked at bookstores, and I wanted to be able to go into my first-year classes that fall and tell people where I worked. I wasn't going to just be some kid from the Avenue of Champions, I was going to be a cultured and learned bookstore employee slash university student. Shit, I thought I might even go get glasses and a sweater-vest or something with my first paycheque.

At Granny's house, I sat by her land-line phone waiting for one of the stores to call. I waited for a day. That turned into another day, which turned into another one. I decided that with my first paycheque I was going to get a cellphone instead of a sweater-vest. Then I wouldn't have to sit there. Granny didn't have voicemail. She didn't want anyone to be able to bug her. Only crooks leave voicemails, she told me once.

I ended up waiting a week before I thought, *Fuck it.* None of the stores called me back, not one, and I had hit up so many for a job. I went back to one of the Chapters locations and wandered the aisles. All the employees looked happy; they were in their black T-shirts, laughing, talking with customers about books, helping them find what they needed. I picked up a book from the shelf, a biography of Che Guevara with a fancy-ass cover. As I flipped through the pages, I noticed a little piece of white paper that had squares on it. I took it out and put it into another book that was on the shelf. Then I slipped the Che Guevara book into my backpack. I walked through the aisles to the fiction section. There, I found the Kerouac books and went through and did the same thing, removed the squares and slipped the books into my bag. I had about five or six in there when I walked out. If the alarm rang, I was going to fucking book it. None of these chumps in their little outfits would be able to catch me, and I doubt any of them would even try. The alarm didn't go off, and no one stopped or even looked at me. I was invisible to them.

After I left the store with my bag full of books, I walked to the nearest used bookstore.

"We can give you forty dollars in store credit or twenty-five dollars in cash for these," the lady behind the counter said.

"I'll take the cash please."

Later that night, I met up with Alex at his aunt's place.

"Dude, that's so sweet, twenty-five bucks for a couple dumb books. Nice," he said.

"Yeah, they're all clueless in there too. Like who the fuck steals from a bookstore and then pawns them off at another one."

"Oh buddy, what if you tried to return them to the same store?" Alex asked.

"I think you need a receipt for something like that," I said.

"Oh yeah. Well shit, that's still awesome."

You couldn't pull it off at Coles or the smaller chains in the neighbourhood malls. There wasn't enough privacy or space, and the staff there were too invasive. Chapters, though, was perfect. They had tons of privacy and customers in them all the time. I'd hit the City Centre Chapters, then the north side, then West Ed, then Westside, then Whyte Ave, and just kept alternating between them.

Later that summer, Alex and I were hanging out at the Kingsway Mall food court. I was crushing a couple TacoTime specials and he had a plate full of perogies. There were a couple really beautiful ladies sitting next to us. They both had drinks from Orange Julius and were wearing Gap name tags. Alex and I kept talking louder and louder about some party he had been at last weekend, hoping that the ladies would notice us and think we were tough and cool or something. But they just got up and left.

"Let's go get jobs at the Gap," I said as they walked away.

"Hell yeah," Alex replied.

We walked into the Gap and filled out a couple applications. They must have been desperate or something because afterwards the manager brought us into the backroom and gave us an interview right then and there. I spoke for most of it; I didn't want Alex to blow it by saying something that betrayed our Avenue of Champions background.

Alex and I came back the next day for training. We had to change out of our black hoodies and jeans and wear Gap clothes. Alex picked out a pair of dressy khakis and a button-up shirt. I grabbed a pair of cords and a sweater-vest. I still wanted one to show off that I was going to university.

"You look like an old dork," Alex said, laughing at my outfit.

"So do you. Nice button-up. 'Hi, my name's Alex, I do business,'" I replied.

The manager showed us how to properly fold clothes, which we promptly forgot. Then we learned how to remove the security tags by swiping them over this little deactivation pad that sat by the till. On the first day, we were supposed to follow around one of the other staff members and learn the key buzzwords they used to sell clothes. Everyone who comes in the store is looking for something, the manager told us.

The store policy was that when the shift change happened, they would check everyone's bag to make sure no one had any Gap items inside. The manager was really proud that her Gap location had zero shoplifting problems and always had a full inventory. Alex and I saw this as a challenge. We forgot about our original reason for getting jobs there, which was to try and chat with the ladies we saw in the food court. Stealing clothes was going to be our new game.

I thought up this move. I grabbed one of the messenger bags and deactivated the sensor on it. That was the hardest part of the whole move, because you didn't need to fold the bag or anything. So I really had no reason to bring it up to the till. When Alex or I walked by, the lady who worked behind the till—one of the women we saw in the food court—wouldn't even look in our direction. I took advantage of this and quickly swiped the bag over the deactivation pad when she turned her back on us. Then I put it back where it normally went, but behind the other bags so that a customer wouldn't grab it. When Alex and I had to fold clothes during our shift, we just brought them up to the till and folded them on the counter. While we were doing a terrible job folding them, we swiped the clothes over the deactivation pad. When we brought them back out to the floor, instead of putting them back in their spots, we just shoved them in the hidden messenger bag. Right before our end-of-shift meeting, I moved the bag, placing it right beside the exit. During the meeting, the manager went over the sales numbers from the shift, gave out an award to the employee whose name was mentioned the most at the register, then checked all our bags and dismissed us. Alex and I proudly presented our empty backpacks. Alex stayed behind to ask the manager a bunch of distracting questions. I followed the rest of the employees as they left, making sure that I was the last one. When I went by where the bag was sitting, I grabbed it, shouldered it and walked out.

"These clothes are lame as shit. We should get jobs at West49 or something," Alex said. We were going through the messenger bag.

"I don't even know who would buy these from us," I said.

"Ah whatever, maybe my uncle or someone else wants them," Alex replied.

"I guess I could wait until university and try to sell them to kids in my class or something," I said.

"That's a good call, we'd get the shit beat out of us if we were wearing these around the Avenue."

Alex and I lasted two more shifts. We filled up a bag on each one, then we just stopped showing up. I don't even think we picked up our paycheques for those three shifts, we just forgot about them and started stealing bikes instead.

* * *

"So, where are you thinking about applying?" Cheryl asked.

"Well, I don't really like retail, or grocery stores, and with prepay, pumping gas isn't really a thing anymore," I said. I shrugged my shoulders. "I really don't know."

"What about a coffee shop or a bar or something?" she suggested.

"Coffee shops sound so boring," I said. "You'd have to sit there, listening to whiny white dudes singing folk songs about how hard life is in the suburbs. Blah."

"Then get a serving job, you dumb-ass," Cheryl said. "I'm just trying to help."

"Maybe I'll apply at your pub," I said.

"Not a chance."

"I'm nice, charming and funny. I could probably make bank serving," I said.

"Don't forget modest too," Cheryl replied.

6. PRAIRIE

There are bed bugs in my apartment building, so we have to flee fucking post-haste. I pack my roommate's cat up in her little crate and hop into my inheritance from old Aunty Doreen, a blue '98 Chevy Lumina. We barely make it out before they have the white-and-blue bubble wrap covering the building and the chemicals pumping in. The landlords told us about five minutes before all these exterminators arrived looking like astronauts and stomping around the building. "Push everything out from the walls," they kept yelling, like we had all the time in the world. I think the plumber yelled the same thing last time the building flooded. We're ground floor, too, so all the shit from the three storeys above us floods in. I told the landlords to call a fucking plumber a few days beforehand when the sink was gurgling and spitting, but nope, they couldn't understand what I was saying. Wasn't speaking in dollars. But shit, what can you do? It's all slumlords everywhere. An English prof told me once that Thomas King wrote about stories and how it's all turtles all the way down. Well this is slumlords. It's fucking slumlords all the way down.

I drive my car from the Avenue of Champs down to the university area. Thank God I put some change in the gas tank on Monday, discount day at the Domo. It's cold, like my balls have gone back inside my stomach cold. The cat's purring away in her little crate.

Prairie and I make it to campus and people are looking at me like, *What the fuck, why is this guy walking through the humanities building carrying a cat?* And I see them snickering. All the other students without cats in crates. And it occurs to me for the first time that this may have been a bad idea; I didn't think it through, I never think about it, unfortunately, until it's too late. But fuck it, I smile back. I got nowhere else to go and I don't want this cat to get fumigated or freeze to death in my car, so we're both gonna hit up my Indigenous literatures class. The cat might get more out of it than I will. Because right now I don't know where those turtles are.

"Why do you have a cat with you?" Professor Gladue asks me.

"Why wouldn't I have a cat with me?" is what I wish I had the confidence to say. Instead I mumble something along the lines of, "I'm sorry, I can leave if you want."

"No, it's fine, just sit in the back," she replies with a sigh. I head to the back and take a seat as she instructs. Professor Gladue is very intimidating. Knows a lot about everything related to Natives and, I assume, everything else. She's from out east, some 'Nish rez, I think. Though there are Gladues all over this area. Part of me wishes—okay, all of me wishes—that I had my shit together and could impress her with a story or a poem or something. Instead I've got a cat and half a pack of Canadian Goose smokes.

No one sits by me. But no one ever does. I'm straight up *that* kid. I used to be popular back in our ghetto-ass high school and during summers back at Buffalo Pound. That kind of popularity doesn't translate to university, though. Here it's all about the money and not being the smelly guy, reeking like old cigarettes, plastic-bottle whisky and Old Milwaukees, and carrying a cat. Who's thinking, *That dude's the shit*, when I'm carrying a fucking cat around? Prairie's cool with no one hanging by us though. She just chills, purrs a bit, then goes to sleep. Makes me wish someone was carrying me around. I'd reverse our roles in a heartbeat. Then I think, *Shit, I just wish I had somewhere or someone to go to right now.* But I don't.

Class goes by slow. I can barely concentrate on the best of days. Today is not one of them and I spend most of the class sticking my fingers through the crate door trying to pet Prairie. She's having a great time, all snuggled up and purring away in her sleep, just out of reach of my flailing fingers. I want to open the cage up and pull her into my lap, but I think that might be the last straw with the prof and that would be the end of my university experience. The other students in the class ignore me and I watch as they put up their hands and answer question after question.

Professor Gladue watches the students as they drone on. I watch her watch the students. She ignores me. The cat continues to snore-purr, ignoring everyone.

Class ends and I have nothing else to do for the day. I step outside the humanities building for my after-class smoke, just to feel that the sun hasn't warmed anything up and it's still biting cold. I had been entertaining the idea of sleeping in my car but in this temperature we'd be dead before morning. The cat wakes up and I let her out of her crate to run around on the frozen ground. The cement freezes her paws and she darts back into the crate. I realize that I forgot to grab cat food in the mad dash. My bank account is reading really low, so I'm hoping that the cat will eat some leftovers I can scrounge up from the garbage cans around the university. I guess if worse comes to worst I can try and steal some food for the cat from the grocery store down the block. I'll be fine. It isn't my first time going without for a few days and I'm not above my classmates' leftovers. Never have been, not going to start now. Last time the building was getting fumigated, they made us stay out for three days. I'm assuming that's our timeline this round, too. No one said otherwise, not that they would—those shady fucks, they don't give a shit. They would probably prefer if none of us ever came back to the building so they could just live in this weird little fumigated slumlord kingdom with no slummies to worry about.

Prairie and I find some food, then we set up shop down in the library computer area. I don't have my own computer, so I use this forced time at the university to actually do some homework for once. It's getting late and the library is getting down to the weirdos. There's some old guy watching dude on dude porn in the corner. His computer screen is just one big cock with another guy's hand stroking it. A crew of engineering students are playing video games a couple computers away from him. I'm sitting here with a cat. We're a motley crew. Each time the cat shifts in her crate, I start thinking she's going to start losing it, since she's been in this box for most of the day. I want to lose it and I haven't even been in a box, at least not one this confining. There's an offset room, one of those study ones that students can use. I roll in there with Prairie and let her out again. First thing, I turn off the lights. Hopefully security will be lazy tonight and not do proper rounds. It's so fucking cold outside. I really don't want to sleep in the car. If you sleep in the car, you wake up just fucking frozen. I don't have enough gas to run the car all night to keep the heat going either.

Prairie scurries around a bit checking out the new digs. It's a small room. Just a round table and six chairs. I push one of the chairs up against the door handle. A little security in case someone does try to get in here. Maybe they'll get the hint if the door doesn't open. I stretch out under the table and start cruising through my textbook from Professor Gladue's class looking for examples of conflict between tricksters and the other characters.

The door slams open and the chair goes flying against the side of the wall with a crash. There's a flashlight on my face and the lights scream on.

"Is that a fucking cat?" I hear a voice yell. Some dude jumps on me and presses his knee into my throat. "What are you doing in here?" the knee asks.

"I'm a student. Shit, I just fell asleep."

"Do you have identification?" Knee presses harder into me.

"Relax. Fuck. It's in my pocket. Can you get the fuck off me?" The knee lets up but he keeps a lock on me. There's a second security guard in the doorway blocking any chance to run. They both look like cop school dropouts but are still trying to play the game, moustaches and the whole nine yards. I see Prairie in the corner checking it all out. She's got her hackles up.

What if she jumps up and scratches the shit out of this dude? What would he do? It would be funny as hell, but he'd probably smash her. I didn't want that at all. I reach into my back pocket and pull out my student ID card.

"See, I'm a fucking student."

"Well, you can't be sleeping here."

"Where the hell else am I going to go? It's fucking cold out there, man."

"A lot of people sleep in that Tim Hortons by the hospital."

The security guard releases his grip on me. I walk over to grab Prairie and put her in the crate.

"You can't be in here anymore. You need to leave campus."

"What if I start studying or something?"

"No, you need to leave now."

I grab my backpack and the crate and start walking out of the library. There are still a few students at the twenty-four-hour computers. They've all turned to look at me. The old dude and his porn are long gone. *I should have just fucking sat at one of those computers,* I think to myself. A couple students are sleeping on couches by the entrance.

"What about those guys?" I ask security.

"They're studying."

Security walks me off campus.

Inside the Tim Hortons, a cat is the least of anyone's worries. It's packed in there. One side of the eating area has been completely taken over by homeless people. They're spread out on the benches and on the floor, under tables and in the aisles. Prairie and I find a spot under one of the only free tables and settle in. I use my backpack as a pillow. It's uncomfortable as fuck and the floor is sticky, covered in something that's definitely not double-double. But shit, it could be, too. At this point, I'm tired and my mind is clogged from eating only scraps and smoking cigarettes all day. I put Prairie right next to me. I'm not worried about anyone taking her since everyone here has their own problems to deal with. At this moment, we all just want to get through the night and this cat is the only thing bringing me any sort of comfort.

I never truly sleep in a situation like this. I'll get a bit of rest and then I'm awake again, constant vigilance, you know. Never comfortable. Cold and sticky, fluorescent lights burning down, and a stream of people from the university hospital and kids from the residence buildings coming in for coffees and Timbits. They all avoid looking at our little camp. Which is probably for the best, as I don't want to see anyone I might be in a class with. It's already embarrassing enough having a cat in class. Now I have a cat and I'm sleeping on the floor of the Tim Hortons. Classic fuck-up right here.

One of the boys sleeping on the bench above me rolls over and belches. His breath is full of old nicotine and cold french fries and goes right into my nose.

"Rest up kid, they're gonna come in and boot us out of here at six," he says to me.

I roll over and face the other way, but it's more uncomfortable on my side so I'm back on my back in a second staring at the underside of the table. At least we've got a few hours, I think to myself. French fry breath starts snoring above me.

"Daniel, is that you?"

I close my eyes tighter. It's just a dream. It's just Prairie talking to me.

"Daniel. What are you doing?"

I know the voice, it's Professor Gladue from Indigenous lit. I open my eyes. She's standing there a good ten feet away from the homeless area. With her are two guys and a lady. They all look fancy and clean, even though they're just wearing winter coats and wool toques. But they're those coats that are brown wool and have nice collars. None of them are doubling up on hoodies and wearing beer-box freebie toques. They all just look clean: clean beards, clean hair, clean. I don't think they have bed bugs or lice or fleas or meth-heads running around in their buildings.

"Hey," I say.

"Are you okay? Do you need anything?" she asks. Her voice sounds different than it does in class. Less authoritative, friendlier, not hollow.

"Nah, I'm good." Her crew are all staring at me. Their eyes are full of pity. "I'll see you in class. Thanks."

"Is the cat with you?" she asks.

"Oh, yeah, right here." I pat the hoodie draped over Prairie's crate.

"Okay," she says. Her crew starts walking toward the door. She follows them and at the last minute turns around and looks back at me. I'm trying to pretend I'm already asleep but I notice. And I'm thinking how fucked I am for next class now. She's going to think I'm a real piece of shit. She's not going to take a word that I write for the essay seriously. This is done. It's too late in the semester to drop though, so I'll have to take the F. With the academic probation shit, that'll boot me out of school. But hell, it was never meant to be anyways. I close my eyes. Six a.m. comes too early in the winter. I can hear Prairie softly purring from inside her crate. She seems comfy, carefree, cozy. I would give anything to be able to crawl inside that crate with her and cuddle up.

7. GRADUATION

Being inside a building feels unnatural to me. It's just those lights, just staring right through everything, exposing every little hair and freckle. The air, too. That stale, stagnant air filled with the coughs of thousands of people. Pass. I'll take my life outside please. That's the best thing about working on the high-rises. We never have to go inside. We build the frames, the structures, dance around on the beams, rise slowly into the air one floor at a time. Then boom, we're in the sky, and one of the guys takes a photo from the top. No roofs, no walls, just sky and birds all the way up.

Walking through the door of that building felt like I shoved my head right up a moose butt. Wild, man, how people just spend all their days in these fucking pits. Only other time I went to a university was when I took Daniel to check one out. Now the little fuck is done. That went by fast. I guess I've ridden four or five towers into the sky in the same amount of time. So, really, what's more important, a piece of paper or a bunch of slick-looking towers? Only time I need paper is when I'm in the shitter. Mind you I've never been inside one of those towers; they don't exactly let people like me live in them. Daniel's piece of paper might get him into one now though. That's what happens to people with those papers, they tend to leave and only come back when they need something.

At the graduation ceremony, I can feel all of the people around me trying not to stare too hard. They're doing that thing, moving their eyes every which way but in my general direction. I know they're watching. They're not sure of what to expect from the guy with tattoos from the ears down. I thought the blue collared shirt I picked up at the thrift store would have hidden the tattoos a bit better. First time I think I've ever actually worn a collared shirt. No wait, that's a lie. I wore one at Grandpa's funeral too. It's hard to find shirts that fit me. I'm a big boy. Fuck it, I don't really give a shit what they think. I'll never see any of these people again.

I walk through the hall looking for an aisle seat. Nothing doing, so I end up crawling over a bunch of people who all give me the smile that says, *Why did you pick this row? Who are you trying to convince? Do you really think your big ass is small enough to crawl over us?* I'm hoping the Tim Hortons double-double I chugged before coming in won't make me have to take a leak. I really don't want to have to climb back across the laps of all these people. I'm already feeling like the moose is clenching his butt cheeks and squeezing my head. I don't need their hands shoved up there, too.

They're starting up the graduation or convocation, whatever you call it. The first person talks about Métis and Cree people and treaty land. Everyone in my aisle is side-eyeing me while the speaker does the land acknowledgment, trying to judge what my reaction will be. Then they bring up a Cree Elder. Granny would know what he was saying. Daniel too, probably. Me though, shit I haven't picked up any words besides the ones that everyone, including the white people, know.

Even if Granny still lived in the city, she wouldn't have come to Daniel's graduation with me. She still won't go near a hospital, school, brick building, anything really. Not big on authority, that old lady. Before I left my apartment to catch the train down to the university she called and told me to be careful. She's never told me anything like that in my goddamned life. This coming from the same lady who legit tried to get me to drop out of school when I turned twelve. And then when I did drop out when I was fifteen or sixteen—can't remember—well, she thought that was better than graduating. Be careful? All these assholes staring at me should be careful, not me. They remind me of the kids back in school who would always scream, "I'll sue you!" when you'd beat them up. The difference is, though, no one believes a little Métis kid is going to sue anyone. These guys are probably lawyers already and would love nothing more than locking up another big, dumb Métis dude. If I think this university hall is a moose butt, I can't imagine what a jail cell would feel like.

I feel pretty fortunate that I've never been to jail. Most of my buddies have done a bit of time here and there. Most of the guys at work too. All of them have gone in for nothing major— assault, theft, possession with intent, break and enter—things that won't get you much time. I've still got another ten years until all the dudes I know who went in for something heavy get out. There were moments that could have gone either way, don't get me wrong, but somehow I've managed to steer pretty clean. The assaults I've been charged with all got dropped too. Fucks that charged me didn't show up in court, scared shitless I bet, so they just let me walk.

Now I make good bank. I'm not going to get rich. But I make enough to have my little apartment and keep a fridge stocked with beers and whatever I want to eat. I remember one time when we were kids, Granny sent Daniel and I to go grab the usual groceries from the store. She gave us just enough change to pay for the log of bologna and a loaf of white bread. Granny taught us to take the free mustard packs from the deli area. Daniel and I wandered through the aisles, looking at all the food that we'd never get to eat. I remember the two of us standing in the chips and beef jerky aisle. Daniel was staring at a big bag of jerky when he turned to me and said, "I'll know I've made it in life when I can go into a grocery store and buy anything I want and not even look at the price." I thought that was a pretty smart thing for a kid to say. So if that's the bar then I've hit it. I can buy anything I want from the grocery store. Not that I do—I still stick to bologna, mustard and white bread. But every once in a while I'll hammer down a bag of jerky. Spitz too, I like Spitz, especially during ball season.

I don't think I'd do too good with white-dude money. I'd have to leave the Avenue, that's for sure. Or just blow it quickly. Nothing good can happen from having a bank account, RRSPS and TFSAS and mortgages and interests. Every once in a while, a buddy or an ex-girlfriend gets their cows and plows money from the Federales. We'd have wild parties on that cash. People would buy kegs of beer, Texas mickeys, dope, legit cocaine—not the 55 percent baking soda shit that was usually around. We had some good parties. But buddies all knew that they had to get rid of that cash. You can't keep it, or you change, man. You become something else. And what fun would it be to sit there with a bank full of tons of money? The way I see it, you gotta give back to the community. Might mean something different to all these university people here, but to me and my friends, giving back to the community means hosting the party of the year. When I was younger, I thought maybe the Papaschase would get their shit together and I could get in on a federal payout for the government booting Granny's granny off her land. I'm not holding my breath for that anymore though.

I've been sitting here forever. How many kids graduate from a university each year? I don't know if I've ever seen this many people in my entire life. Even at the big inner-city powwow, you don't get this many people in a space. From my seat, all I can see is wave after wave of grey hair and bald domes cheering for their kids when they go across the stage. The cheers for each person come up like little farts from different areas of the hall. I wonder how long I'll have to sit here until Daniel gets to go. He didn't ask me to come or anything. He knows that I'm not a big fan of spaces or places like these. I'm sure he remembers that the last time I went to the university with him, I had to dip. But I wouldn't miss this. How many people do I know that are going to finish a university degree? Let alone that person being my little brother. That shit isn't going to happen again in my lifetime. Even when I have some kids, I wouldn't expect them to get through something like this. Daniel's always been a bit different though. Teachers treated him alright. He didn't have to fight at every turn. He knew how to read. He would even do it back at Granny's, too. Bringing books home from the library and staying up all night on the bottom bunk until he'd finish them. He'd tuck a flashlight that Grandpa gave him in the bunk bed bars so he could get light on the pages without disturbing me. Good kid. Didn't want to disturb me then and didn't want to disturb me now, but nothing's gonna stop me from seeing him walk across that stage.

It helped too that the crew wasn't working today and I didn't have to ask for the day off or anything. We're switching to a new site. We just finished off this big beast, the tallest building in the city. But we're heading right next door where they've already started a building that's going to dwarf this one. I can't comprehend the type of people who would want to live in one of these buildings. I like building them, sure, but to stay up there, that's fucking crazy. I'm sure my boss would have given me the day off. He's pretty good to me but still, I hate to ask something like that. I've been on his crew for a few years now, which is a lot longer than anyone else has lasted. Most people on our crew come in for a few paycheques and then fuck off and we don't see them again. I guess it was a few years back now when I was walking downtown and noticed a *Labourers Wanted* sign hanging on the chain-link fence surrounding a big hole in the ground. I walked over to the trailer and met the man who would become my boss. First thing he says to me is, "Why the fuck should I hire an Indian like you? The last Indian I hired fucked off after his first cheque."

So I told him, "Well how many white dudes have done the same thing?" He just started laughing.

"You got a point," he said. Then he told me to come back the next day with a hard hat and a pair of steel-toes, and that if I needed some there was a careers centre across from the community college that gave them out to Indians.

I'm starting to sweat. It's hot in this hall. The sun outside is starting to beam in through the windows and the old building's cranking up. I'm not used to wearing a collared shirt like this and as I get hotter and hotter it starts constricting around my neck. Some days I miss Granny. She would laugh if she saw me now, all red faced and sweaty, surrounded by moniyaw in a university built on the area that her granny called home. But she's busy playing cards and bingo on the Island. Daniel and his friends had this hilarious weed-dealing scheme. A real dealer would have called it cute. They were able to get away with it because it was so pitiful. No self-respecting dealer was going to waste his time worrying about them for the tiny amounts they were selling. I knew Daniel was giving the profits to Granny, who was growing the dope for him. That's the only reason that I went and scared those kids who mugged Daniel. That was my way of helping out him and Granny.

Finally, Daniel walks across the stage and I don't yell or nothing. I don't want to draw any attention to myself. I watch an old lady step forward and wrap a Métis sash around his waist. She ties it off to the right. I don't recognize the lady but I'm sure Granny would know her. Granny knows everyone. Then they pass him a piece of paper while he shakes hands with a line of people on his way off the stage. After he's done, I crawl over the people in my aisle to get out of there. I'm sure Daniel will be celebrating with his buds, and I don't want to bother them. I'll see him back on the Avenue of Champions.

8. MOSQUITOES

The apartment was covered in blood from ceiling to floor and on every little window, as if a six foot four, 240-pound ballet dancer had been punctured a thousand times by a fillet knife and then spun his way across the living room, through the kitchen and bedroom, finally coming to rest in the bathroom after one final arterial-spurting spin. Jason followed him into the bathroom and watched as the bathtub slowly filled with blood around the big man, now slumped in an unnatural contortion, hair clogging the drain and legs folded out like a spatchcocked duck.

"Pussy! I barely touched you," Jason spat at the dead man. Back in the kitchen, Jason began to wash the blood off his knife. Then he started thinking about where the money might be and forgot the knife, left it sitting in the sink with the water running. The apartment was disgusting before it had been soaked in layers of blood. Now it looked like someone had taken the ketchup packets from the old fast-food bags laying around everywhere and stomped on them. Just like Jason and his cousins used to do in the parking lot of the Burger Baron on the Avenue of Champions, under the fading mural eyes of former Edmonton Eskimos and Oilers. *I could use a beer,* Jason thought. Something to bring him back to that calm feeling that was rolling through him right when he started stabbing. The big dead man didn't have anything in his fridge except expired milk and a grease-soaked pizza box filled with mouldy crusts. Jason went through the cupboards, looking for the money. The fire running through his body was returning and it felt like his veins would explode, releasing the thousand mosquitoes inside his body that were slowly devouring him. It must have been hours since Jason had had his last fix. The mosquitoes had subsided when he entered the apartment through the screen door on the second-floor balcony and stabbed the sleeping man. His only moment of reprieve in the last couple days.

* * *

There used to be no mosquitoes and no bears. Instead there were foster homes, group homes, social workers, cops, teachers, counsellors, more social workers, more group homes, more cops. Jason remembered being dropped off at his aunty's house to "spend the night," as his dad called it. Spending the night meant anywhere from a couple hours to a couple months, depending on what happened to his dad. Jason would sit up all night playing crib with his aunty and she would tell him stories. She talked about how she grew up in a small cabin tucked away in the forest with a view of the Rocky Mountains. How the only heat came from the wood-burning stove, and how it was her job from when she was just a little girl to split wood. How during the long winter nights, the neighbours would come from all over with their fiddles, drums, songs and stories, and stay up all night making music and dancing. How, though they had almost nothing material and food wasn't plentiful, they still felt like they had everything. His aunty told him that she wished Jason's dad had been able to grow up there with her, how if he had been ten years older he would have remembered the beauty in their Métis culture and the stories, always the stories. Instead Jason's dad only knew the city, where the family was forced to move after someone purchased the land. All the stories had an element of beauty. Jason felt at home within his aunty's voice, comforted, warm, part of something. Her stories were different from the stories his dad told him when he got home.

"You should have seen that guy, man. He had all sorts of cash. And he says to me, 'Bring this to Maple Creek. I got ya a Greyhound ticket.' And I know all about Greyhounds so I wander down to that bar across from the station. Order three shots of whisky. Drain the first two. Then I pour the third shot all over me. Know why I did that?"

"Why?" Jason was leaning in, tipping the old lawn chair he was sitting on to a forty-five-degree angle, straining to hear every word his dad stumbled over.

"'Cause you go get that back seat, lay down across 'er and no one will ever bother ya. They come near and just sniff the air, they getting liquored." Jason's dad lit a cigarette and poured himself a glass of potato champagne from the bottle Jason's aunty had in front of her on the table. Jason's dad exhaled a plume of smoke toward the nicotine-stained stucco ceiling.

Jason watched as the smoke swirled up and up and up and he could swear that he saw a Greyhound bus rolling toward a tiny little gas station surrounded by nothing on a cold prairie winter night. "So anyways, I show up in Maple Creek. And I'm standing outside freezing my tits off, it's so cold lighters aren't even working. Had to stuff mine against my nut sack just to keep 'er warm enough to light a smoke. When, fuck me, a cop comes pulling up."

"What?" Jason screeched.

"Yup, a fucking cop." Jason's dad drained the glass and passed it across the table for Aunty to fill up. She filled it to the brim and slid it back across. "You know the RCMP were created to keep us Métis down. Batoche and shit. You know that, right? Never trust a cop. Never trust a cop." He had enough slur on the last word to close his eyes and start inhaling and exhaling on the lit cigarette hanging out of the corner of his mouth. Aunty filled her own glass back up, took an appropriate sip and rolled her eyes.

"ekwayikohk," she said, staring daggers at the top of Jason's dad's head. Jason's dad poked his head back up.

"So the cop comes to me and he goes, 'Chilly eh?' and I'm sitting there like what the fuck man, I got a bag full of fucking grass, I'm wasted off my rocker and standing alone in fucking Maple Creek. I think to myself, you know, I'm going to fucking jail."

"But you're not in jail," Jason yelled. The excitement took hold of him and he stood up and started jumping up and down holding onto the edge of the table.

"Nah, my little man. Cop was the one who was buying the grass. Can you believe?" Jason's dad's head slunk down from one final slur for the night. Not a minute later he began to snore. Aunty took the almost-finished cigarette out of his mouth and stabbed it out.

"Damn, bears. You, time for bed now." Aunty put her hand on Jason's shoulder and steered him toward the sewing room where an old army cot was permanently set up for him.

"Dad going to bed too?" Jason asked.

"Yeah, Dad's going to bed," Aunty muttered.

"I'm glad he didn't go to jail this time," Jason replied. Aunty nodded.

The last time Jason saw his dad, he had just woken up for school. They were back in their apartment. Jason was sitting on the old couch eating a bowl of Shredded Wheat without milk. They didn't have milk unless Aunty or one of his dad's girlfriends brought some over. Jason found a half-empty two-litre of Pepsi in the fridge and a full bag of salt-and-vinegar chips. He threw them in his backpack for lunch and left, with his dad still snoring away on the couch surrounded by empty beer cans and a two-six of Royal Reserve.

Later that morning, Jason was sent down to the principal's office where his aunty was waiting for him with a social worker and a cop. They told Jason that his dad had been arrested and he would be staying with his aunty from now on. Six months later, Aunty was walking home from bingo, as she did every Friday night, when she disappeared. Her friends all saw her leave the hall, but she never showed up back at her place. There wasn't a newspaper article, a police investigation or anything, just an empty presence in Jason's life where his aunty had once been.

For a while, Jason had tried to remember the group homes and the foster homes. He would try to remember his aunty, but just like most of the social workers, she had disappeared into a void of dark shapes in his head. Jason didn't know anything but group homes, foster homes and the hell that occurred in them. He tried so hard not to think about them. Why couldn't they disappear the way the stories had? That's all Jason wanted, to make everything disappear in a haze of pint and cheap wine.

Sometimes he'd let his guard down and talk to some of the women he ran around with about it. They usually had a similar story of abuse and violence, with everything tracing back to Children's Services. He met the women around the drop-in shelters and the tent cities north of downtown. They usually teamed up to try and get their medicines.

"When I was twelve, I stayed with two families, both very white, churchy-type people. They loved bringing me to church. We went every Sunday and sometimes Wednesdays too. I think I was twelve. I mean, I must have been. Or maybe thirteen. I don't know." Jason would pass the pipe over and whatever lady he was with would nod. Sometimes she had her own list. Sometimes they would talk about the group homes they ended up in when they were older. They never talked about their real families, or what became of them. Sometimes they just smoked in silence until the crystals started raining ice through their joints and they had to move. Jason loved fucking when he was high.

"Got bear juice running through me, if you know what I'm saying. Some rabbit root," Jason would say to his girlfriends. The sex happened everywhere when they were moving through the city's alleys and abandoned parks. Every once in a while the rabbit root started becoming too strong and they had to lay down in the bushes and go for it. Jason loved tramping around after they finished howling like dogs. The women became a blur. They were all in it for the same thing, and they just happened to cross paths at the same time. There was no connection besides an immediate need to get rid of the mosquitoes inside their veins.

Jason was walking down the Avenue of Champions toward the walk-up apartment he had been crashing at for the past few weeks. The guy whose name was on the lease had just up and left after a good party night and no landlord had come around yet to check on the spot. By the Avenue Community Centre, a bunch of tents and tipis were set up. People were everywhere. There were food trucks set up, camera crews and bouncy castles. A band with a fiddle player would play one song and then a drum group would play one, they kept alternating back and forth. Jason went and stood over by one of the food trucks and watched the two groups perform. He loved fiddle music. It reminded him of his aunty.

"Jason, what's up man? Is that you?" A pudgy guy wearing a flat-brimmed Oilers cap was walking toward him. He had a hot dog in each hand. "Holy shit dude, how you doing?" Jason shrugged and started to turn around and get out of there. "Dude, it's me, Daniel."

Jason stopped. "Daniel? Shit man. What's up?"

"Man, it's great to see you. Hey, you want one of these?" Daniel eyed him up and down and Jason was sure he was looking into every pockmark and scar on his face.

"Nah, I'm good."

"Come on dude, I don't need two, obviously." Daniel forced a hot dog into Jason's hand and then patted his gut with the other one. "Quit smoking darts and started putting on the pounds."

"Oh yeah?"

"Yeah, no one really smokes in the office I'm working in."

"Yeah, for sure," Jason tried to search his memory. He could not for the life of him remember the last time he saw Daniel. "Look man, you wouldn't mind helping me out a bit, would you? I've had a bad week," he said.

"Of course not. It's great to see you. You doing okay?" Daniel asked as he grabbed a twenty out of his wallet. Jason noticed that there were quite a few in there.

"I'm doing okay. What about you?" Jason asked. He wondered how he could get another one of those twenties from Daniel. May as well keep this conversation rolling.

"Yup, got a job working for the government, doing some Indigenous relations work. Never thought I'd get something like that, you know. Good soniyaw from the moniyaw."

"Hell yeah man," Jason replied.

"You hear about my brother, Charlie? You remember him right?" Daniel asked. Jason nodded. Charlie, he did know. The guy had been a goon around the neighbourhood since they were little kids. He ran into him every so often outside one of the pubs on the Avenue.

"He was over at the River Cree the other weekend. Got loser drunk and put a thousand bucks down on twenty-three red. Fucking crazy thing, the number hit. Walked out of there with thirty-five Gs."

"You serious man? Shit! What wouldn't I do with that? Lucky fuck."

"Yeah, my friend Keesha was serving drinks that night. Only reason I heard about it. I think he's trying to keep it on the down-low. Okay dude, I better get going, I'm here with some work people and they're probably wondering where I put their hot dogs," Daniel said. He passed Jason a business card. "Give me a shout if you need anything, man, my cellphone is on there."

"Sure man, great seeing you and thanks."

As soon as Daniel had disappeared into the crowd, Jason threw the card and hot dog to the ground. Guy was always weak, even back when they were kids. Fat, spoiled, pasty fuck.

* * *

He tore through every single cupboard and then moved over to the living room, where he grabbed the cushions off the couch and threw them around. Dissatisfied with what he found, he ran back to the sink, grabbed the knife and started stabbing the cushions, which were now on the floor, sending white fuzz all over the room. "Fuck me!" he screamed as he kept stabbing and stabbing until he missed the cushion and slammed his hand down into the exposed spring, leaving a gash across his wrist. Jason's blood started spurting, soaking the white fuzz with his own ketchup packet. "FUCK ME!" he yelled again as he dropped the knife, pulled off his tattered green Pilsner shirt and wrapped it around his wrist. Jason laid down on the floor and screamed. In the distance, he could hear angels singing their hallelujah songs the way they had in the church his foster parents used to take him to when he was still a kid. Before he had mosquitoes inside his veins and a bear on his back. The angels were getting closer. This might be the time they finally took him away for good. Jason closed his eyes and waited.

9. A LIGHT IN THE DARKNESS

It seems like a long time ago since the last time someone called me Patsy. I don't remember when I first started becoming Granny. It must have been after Charlie was born, maybe even when his mother, my baby girl, was pregnant with him. She was a beauty, too beautiful for this world, and much like her boy Charlie, she was born three generations too late and these Prairie cities ate her alive. I hope she's doing well in Vancouver. I haven't seen or heard an owl hoot in years, so she must be okay. Escaping this city may have been the best thing that ever happened to her. But that too was so long ago now that I can only remember the way she stood in doorways, always leaning against them, never just standing up straight. The curls in her hair were always getting tangled around doorknobs or getting dipped into hamburger soup, that's how long her hair was. Not like my stubby old curls here. I removed all her pictures from the house when Children's Services finally gave me custody of Charlie and Daniel. I didn't want the boys to see her when they came to live with their grandpa and me. If they ever asked, I would have brought the box out to show them, but they never did.

My first roommate called me Pat. I preferred Pat to Patsy. It sounded tough. That's what I wanted to be when I came to the city—tough—and not scared of all the buildings and people everywhere. The name Pat helped a bit with that. I felt proud when I introduced myself to people. It was a name no one would mess with. Patsy, on the other hand, was weak. Patsy wasn't able to keep the mounties from burning down her granny's cabin and beating her to within an inch of her life. Patsy wasn't able to keep Uncle Jim from going through the ice. Patsy wasn't able to help. She couldn't do anything. That was part of the reason I came to the city. After the mounties torched the cabin, Granny and I had to move into my parents' place. There was a buttload of little shits running around everywhere in that one-bedroom shack and not enough space to even sit down, let alone have any privacy. As a fifteen-year-old woman, I thought, to hell with that noise, and my dad hitched up his wagon and we took off to the city.

I had an older sister who was already living in the city. She met a good Ukrainian boy when she was working as a teacher. He dealt a good hand of cards and worked on the railroad. She was about to pop out her first kid, and had asked if I wanted to come and help her with it. I didn't know a thing about kids, but I thought that one should be easier to handle than the ten that were screaming all around me in my parents' shack. The Ukrainian boy made good money and could even pay me a little bit. That cash plus a room—hell, life was good. I felt bad abandoning Granny back in that shack with all the kids. But she needed time to heal, and my mom had the knowledge of the proper medicines from the bush that Granny would need to get well again. I knew a bit, but really, I was just starting to learn from Granny. Making moonshine, though, was a skill that she had already taught me.

There was no mixed-gender drinking back in the bars in those days. Booze was a lot harder to come by, and it was priced so high that no working person could get their hands on it. I liked the fact that I could wander down to the Strathcona Hotel and have a drink without any men bothering me. You still had to watch out though. A couple old perverts would always be posted outside the doors, just hoping that some drunk lady would take pity on them, or be so drunk that they could have their way with her. The bartender would chase them off every once in a while, but they'd never go far. If they let those weirdos inside the bar, it would be a whole different story. The perverts didn't go into the lobby of the hotel though. That was where all the married men hung out, waiting for their wives to get out of the bar. When the door would swing open, they would all start hollering at their wives to come home and make them dinner. It was quite funny, dead silence, then a door would open and men's voices would yell into the bar.

"Fuck that," I remember one of the ladies sitting next to me saying. "If he could get his pecker hard then I'd make him dinner. But until then he's on his own and I'll get my kicks right here."

"Let the bastards starve," another lady said.

My sister was busy with the baby, so she wouldn't come down to the bar with me. She also told me that she got hassled in there because she looked too Cree. Me though, I could put on some lipstick, toss my hair up, wear a nice dress and no one would think twice. I did get asked if I was Italian once or twice, Ukrainian too. I would always just smile and laugh at those questions. Granny couldn't care less about a lot of things, but the one thing she always stressed was that we had to be proud to be Métis.

"A lot of good people got shot up by the mounties. You make sure you always honour them, my girl," she said as we drank tea into the long winter nights. Her family had been living on the Papaschase Reserve when the 1885 Resistance broke out. Granny was just a little girl then. A couple of her uncles slipped out from under the eyes of the Indian agent to go and join in with Riel. They never made it back to the Papaschase Reserve. Not long after that, the government forced them all to leave their homes and Granny's family moved up to the bush north of St. Lina. I tried to find out where the reserve would have been from the Strathcona Hotel. I figured you had to walk east until you got to the ravine. Sometimes, after I had a few drinks, I would walk down there until I got to the bridge that crossed over it. I would stand on the top and stare down into the creek, half expecting to see Granny and her family sitting down there in an old shanty, playing fiddle, singing and chatting the night away.

I met my roommate, the lady who started calling me Pat, in the Strathcona Hotel. Turned out that I wasn't much of a help with the baby and my sister had it under control. The tiny apartment that we were all living in was a bit cramped for the four of us. We had a curtain hanging between our beds. The flimsy

sheet didn't do anything to keep the sounds out as the Ukrainian boy and my sister went about making their next kid. That
was part of the reason I would head down to the bar so often.
I hoped that they would be done by the time I got home. But
they were really into it, and it would often go late into the night.
I figured getting my own apartment wouldn't be the worst
thing. Plus, I wouldn't mind doing some fooling around myself.
The lady who would become my roommate had a similar situation. She worked down at the cleaners' and could get me a job.
I was sold on both of those things. We found an apartment two
blocks north of the hotel. It was a one bedroom, but spacious
enough that we were able to use half the living room as my bedroom while she took the bedroom. I'd never lived in any place
like that before. I had privacy. No one was snoring next to me
while I was sleeping. The only farts stinking up the room were
my own.

I started working at the cleaners' with my roommate right
away and we settled into a nice groove. We'd finish our shift at
3:30 p.m., walk home, change into nicer clothes and get done up
enough to get into the bar for an after-work drink. I often forget that, at that point, I was well under the legal age of twenty-
one. My roommate was a bit older but still well under the legal
age. But the bartender didn't seem to care as long as I didn't
look super young. Hence the fancy clothes. After the drink,
we'd head back to the apartment where we'd take turns cooking
meals and doing the dishes. My staples were always soups and
stews. Granny had taught me how to stretch a piece of meat
over a few meals. Soups and stews helped with that. My roommate was a bit fancier; she'd often cook pasta. I had never had

anything like that before. I felt like my stomach was on a fast horse to heaven the first time I had it with her. Tomato sauce and noodles, that was where it was at. After supper, my roommate might read, I'd do some beading, and then we'd be out for the night. This was our routine for the next few years. We'd have boyfriends sometimes, but they came and went. I can't even remember them now. What really mattered was our little apartment and how we had made it our private space.

The summers were hard on me. I missed berry-picking camp. That was my favourite time of the year. My father would hitch up the wagon and load Granny, my mother and all of the girls into it, myself included. We'd set off for the spot that Granny had designated for us for that year. The spots rotated on a four-year cycle, but if a fire, drought or something else happened they might change again completely. I was never sure how Granny decided where we were going, but I don't remember ever having a lack of berries to pick. My father would help string up sheets in the trees that we would use as our makeshift tent. My mother would take out all sorts of baskets, pails, containers, really anything that could be filled to the brim with berries. Granny would give each of us girls one of the pails. My little sisters would get the smaller ones, me and my older sister would get these big buckets. Off we'd go into the saskatoon bushes that covered the hillsides. We'd spend days out there picking, picking, picking. The younger girls would get bored after filling their pails and they'd run around playing. They'd get all excited about the purple stains on their hands and start using them to make face paint or to draw pictures on their clothes. My older sister would fill her big bucket up once and then help mother with the cooking, cleaning up the berry-stained kids and taking care of the really little ones. But Granny and I, we could go all day.

I've never seen anyone clean the berries off a tree limb like Granny could. She wouldn't leave one saskatoon left on a bush. She'd clean each bush right out and then move on to the next one. Even when I tried that, I'd still end up missing a bunch of them under a leaf or hidden close to the ground or something. And Granny could move, too; she could clean three bushes right out in the time it would take me to do one. She could pick enough saskatoons that her hands would be stained permanently purple until the next season. All the saskatoons would be going back to get canned. They were often the only thing that got us through the winters without all of us getting sick. Those berries—still, to this day, I can't get enough of them.

At night, Granny would tell ghost stories to the kids. Before the story started, she would pour herself a little glass of the moonshine that she brought with her. Then she'd hand me her gun and a shell, and tell me to go hide on the edge of the camp, just off in the woods where my siblings couldn't see me, but I'd still be able to hear the stories.

"You remember all the cues I told you about?" Granny asked.

"Got it," I replied.

I'd settle on the grass and lean up against a stump. I never felt scared or anything being off in the dark bush alone like that, but even then, I'd load the gun up just to be sure, you know. Okay, maybe I was a little scared. But as I listened to Granny's voice carry, I found myself right in the story.

"A long time ago, there was a wee old little lady. This old lady, oh boy, did she have kids. So many kids, there would be three or four times as many as we have here. She lived all alone, way off in the bush all by herself with her kids in a tiny little cabin. The old lady was so far back in the bush that light struggled to get in, and her and the kids got used to being in darkness all the time. But in their cabin they had a nice stove, lots of wood and enough moose meat and berries to live forever. The kids all got along. They loved to play, sing and dance. They were very happy. But then..." Granny paused and took a sip of her moonshine. "Then all sorts of strange things started happening. They began to hear a whistle softly blowing on the wind. At first, they could only hear it when the wind came in from the east. But soon the whistle was on the west wind. It started getting louder and louder. Eventually they all got used to it and started forgetting about the whistle. It didn't take long, though, until the kids started disappearing. At first, it was the oldest boy. 'Good,' the old lady told her other kids. 'He must have gone out into the world to make his way.' Then the next oldest kid was gone. Soon, every night, a new kid was gone. Was something, or someone, taking them? What could it be? The old lady knew she had to do something. She loved her kids, every one of them, and she didn't want any more to disappear. So the old lady, she figured that she would stay up all night and watch for what was coming to take her kids. She made sure to stoke up a big fire in the wood-burning stove. If she was going to be up all night, she may as well be warm. Then she got her gun ready. She waited all night while all around her on the floor her little ones were spread out sleeping. She sat in the middle of the cabin on an old chair next to the stove. She waited. And she waited. And she waited some more. Finally, out of the darkness the whistle started getting louder."

I knew this was my first cue, and I let rip a whistle. I could hear some of my sisters shriek.

"Then, through the door burst a man," Granny continued. "But this wasn't any ordinary man. He was dressed all in black. 'I'VE COME FOR YOUR CHILDREN,' he yelled at the old lady. The old lady tried to shoot the man."

That was my other cue. *BOOM.* I fired the rifle into the air. My siblings were now freaking out.

"But nothing happened. The man kept walking toward her. His strides were long and his black robes started enveloping the room, taking all the light of the wood-burning stove with it. 'Quick! My children, get in here. It's the only way,' the old lady shrieked. 'I promise you'll all be alright.' She opened the door of the wood stove and her children started piling into it one after the other. When her last child had gone into the stove she turned to the man and said, 'We'll always be the light to your darkness.' Then the old lady threw herself into the stove. You could hear a howl coming from the man in the cabin."

I let out a howl.

"But above the cabin, the stars were twinkling in the night sky where there had only been darkness before. And if you counted the stars you would know that each one matched up with one of the old lady's children. And the largest star, well, that was all her. Up in the sky they can dance and sing and be together forever. They never have to be in the darkness."

"Alright, now, bedtime for all of you," my mother interrupted.

My parents started coming into the city more often. They were looking for work. The bush life north of St. Lina was dying out and they needed more money to support their kids. My father and mother hadn't taken up moonshining with Granny, so the one source of steady income that our family had always had was gone. Everyone was hungry and things weren't looking good for the winter. I took to sending them a bit of the cash I made. Then my parents showed up one day with Granny. They let her out at my apartment and took off back to the bush without saying goodbye.

I came home from work and there was Granny sitting under a spruce tree outside the apartment building. She shot right up when she saw me walking down the street. She looked small, smaller than I remembered her. I tried to think back to the last time I'd seen her. My mind was drawing a blank. I ran up to her and gave her a big hug.

"tanisi nosisim iskwesis," Granny said. "You look like a moniyaskwew."

I burst out laughing. "namoya, it's just these fancy clothes," I said. I was wearing the white coveralls that we had to have on in the cleaners' to make sure chemicals didn't splatter all over our skin. "I'm still a good bush girl, you know."

"You'll always be a good bush girl." Granny let go of the hug. "Come now, you need to make me a tea. I've travelled a long way."

We went inside the apartment. Granny looked around, sat in each chair, laid down on the bed, opened every cupboard, went through every little thing.

"You have a fancy life here," she said.

"It's been good. A lot of this stuff is my roommate's," I replied.

"That's good. You don't need all this stuff." Granny opened the closet. She frowned with her eyebrows, then closed the closet door, came back and sat down.

"No potato champagne?" she asked.

"No, sorry. What're you doing in the city?" I asked.

"Visiting. You should make some potato champagne. What if you have visitors?"

I was surprised by the visit. Granny wasn't one for visiting. Especially if she had to go into the city to do it. Her comments about the potato champagne surprised me less.

"No, I'm just kidding you," she said. Her dark-brown eyes twinkled. "We're moving here. Your parents dropped me off and went back to get all the kids."

"You're moving to the city?" I asked.

"What choice do I have? I'm an old lady now. The bush is no place for an old lady without any family around," Granny replied.

"I'll come back and stay with you. I don't need to be here," I said.

"namoya, nosisim iskewsis. You have your life here now. I don't want you taking care of some notokesiw." Granny took a sip of her tea and lit a cigarette. "Besides, we have work to do."

We talked into the night. My roommate had been spending the nights with her new boyfriend, so we didn't see her. Granny had healed up alright from an earlier encounter with the mounties, but she couldn't get back the equipment she needed to really make moonshine. That was all destroyed by the mounties. She took to making homebrew, but it was tough to make a living off just that. People wanted moonshine, and there were other moonshiners who popped up to take Granny's place. Granny still received gifts from some of the local families who would come in and get her to help them out with whatever was troubling or ailing them. She spent a lot of her time making poultices and teas, and helping out when babies were born. The cabin sounded chaotic. At some point, I fell asleep on the couch and Granny in her chair.

The next morning, I woke with the magpies cawing and cackling outside the window. Granny was already up. She sat at the kitchen table smoking and drinking tea. I crawled out of bed and sat down beside her. She got up, poured a cup of tea from the pot, passed it to me, then sat back down. We drank our tea in silence, listening to the birds. After the cups were empty, Granny stood up.

"We need to go," she said. I followed her out of the apartment. It was a beautiful fall morning. The air was crisp, but not yet cold enough to really drop the leaves off the trees. Granny started walking north from the apartment building toward the river.

"Where are we going?" I asked. She didn't respond. For a little old lady, she could sure walk fast. It took everything I had just to keep up with her. Old lady bush strength, my father called it. It was only a couple blocks until we started descending into the River Valley. Granny followed the trails that the City had built until we hit the river's edge. It was running shallow, the rising sun glistened off every ripple of the crystal-clear water. A few old fat mallards were flying around, their tail curls evident in the light and their heads shining purples and greens. I sat down on a rock and looked out at downtown on the opposite shore, the north side of the river. Granny walked right up to the water's edge and stared across.

"Right over there." Granny pointed with her lips to where the Walterdale Bridge entered the flats on the other shore. "That's where we used to set up camp when I was a little one. In the spring and summer when the water was high, we'd canoe or take one of the ferries across the river. When it was this time of year, we could wade across, or ride the horses. There was no big building here," she gestured toward the legislature building. "It was just the fort, where we would buy supplies and trade goods. It was exciting for us as kids to come across to the other side of the river. There were more moniyaw over here, more things to see, and they were starting to build all these buildings." Once again she pointed with her lips at the downtown skyline.

"Where'd you stay?" I asked her.

"Come, my girl." Granny stood up and started walking east. She followed the trails that ran along the riverbank. When we walked under the Walterdale Bridge, she turned to me and said, "This is where I was born." She sat down on the ground. "We were on our way across the river when my mother went into labour. She gave birth to me right here." She patted the soil. "My blood and my mother's blood are bound with the land here. There is nothing else but us. Every step we take, we are walking on the bones and blood of our relatives. Every leaf that crunches under our feet is our ancestors telling us we are home." We walked until we got to where the Mill Creek entered the river. Then Granny turned and started walking up the creek's bank, heading south toward the bridge where I had looked down into the ravine. Soon, we came to railway tracks, which we followed up to an old abandoned shantytown. Not much was left of it. It had been stripped clean of most of the salvageable lumber and parts.

"It was somewhere around here," Granny said. "None of this was here though. It's hard to remember when it's all changed so much."

"How old were you the last time you were here?" I asked.

"I don't remember. Very young. I was just a little girl when the mounties came in and burned down our homes and told us we had to leave. That was the last time I saw lots of our family. They went every which way. But I do remember them still. I remember sitting with them and hearing them sing into the night. They told stories of rivers and lakes and waves the size of bison crashing down on their canoes. Oh, how I loved to hear their stories. Then they were gone. We were all gone." Granny paused. She sat still. I didn't say anything. We just listened.

"You remember, my girl," Granny said. "You remember all of this. These stories need to be told. If they're not, then we are lost as people. All we are is memory and story. When that's gone, then we are just the land, and that's okay, too. It'll be as it should be."

We walked back down to the river and sat on the bank for the rest of the day. As darkness approached, the buildings' lights started coming on. I remembered Granny's story about how each light in the night sky was one of the children. To me, each one of the building lights was one of the children, dancing forever, a light in the darkness.

My parents came back a few days later and picked Granny up. They moved her into their house on the north side and she never came south again. I would go up and visit her regularly over the years. But it was hard, the house was filled with my parents' screaming children, and then soon, the children of the children. My father got a job in the sewers and my mother tended the home. Granny spent most of her time making homebrew and beading. Though she still needed the help of the young children to thread the needle. I'd feel bad when I left their house. Granny was all alone in the mess of children, chaos and noise. She never had much in her life and to end it like this, well, it just seemed sad to me. I'd often cry while I rode the bus back to my apartment. It was getting harder and harder to remember the Granny of my youth. I realized that I knew the concrete better than I knew the trees or the bush. That all seemed so distant. Memories of concrete and the city started stacking up, pushing out all that I had known during my childhood.

We never talked about Uncle Jim. No one did. My family didn't talk much about death, or about people who'd left. Death just seemed to be a fixture in our lives. I never once heard my parents mention Uncle Jim and I sure as shit didn't hear Granny talk about it. All my little brothers and sisters were too young to really remember him or notice his absence. He had always been a character who carried nothing on his shoulders, and left less than when he started. The traces of him in this world were small. There was nothing to remind us of his presence in my parents' cabin after he went through the ice. He wasn't a man who believed in material possessions, nor did he ever have the means to accumulate them even if he'd wanted to. Uncle Jim, much like Granny, could leave in a heartbeat and didn't think twice about it. Wolves moving through the darkness of night. I try to picture Granny mourning Uncle Jim. But the idea of her being sad, or remorseful, or even thinking about it at all, just seemed so out of character for her. I'm sure she did have her own way. But it wasn't one that I knew about. When I think about the two of them now, I like to picture Granny sitting at the little table in her cabin, a mug of Labrador tea steaming in front of her. Uncle Jim would be propped up on the floor, swigging away at his bottle of homebrew, and smoking rollies back to back. Outside, coyotes would be howling, answered in turn by the dogs that always seemed to be hanging around the cabin.

I carried weight in a different way than Granny.

Granny would have loved Charlie and Daniel. She did meet my daughter, but oh, my girl was very, very young then. Just a wee little one, and Granny held her in her arms and stared love into her eyes. I forgot to tell my girl about Granny and the stories. Maybe that's one of the many reasons I failed as a mother. I should have made her prouder of her history, her people. I shouldn't have assumed that she would take that for granted, that she wouldn't have known the beauty and the songs of her Métis culture. Maybe then I wouldn't have lost her to the cities. They would have all done well in a different time, Charlie, Grandpa, my girl, Granny, even Daniel. But the cities. One day we're all young, listening to our uncles tell a story, and the next, we wake up old with skyscrapers all around us. All in one lifetime. What kind of world is that? Why can't it be slow?

I don't know when I became Granny. One morning I woke up as Pat, then the next I woke up as Granny. It wasn't that confusing for my boys, Charlie and Daniel, because they didn't know any other grannies besides me. They didn't know my granny and how she lived. They just heard me tell stories about her. I wasn't going to make the same mistakes with those boys that I had made with my daughter. I want them to know who they are. I want them to be proud. My Granny's been gone a long time now. Ninety-three years old, and she was still jigging, drinking, fighting and singing away until the morning that she decided she wasn't going to wake up again. They had a funeral service for her and they buried her in a cemetery up on the north side of the city. She would have preferred to be dumped in the river. At the service, they played all sorts of old Catholic songs and hymns and prayers, basically all the shit that Granny hated. I sat in the back of the church, as far away from the religion as I could get while still showing my respects. After it was all done, I walked home to the south side. It took about four hours and I set my pace to the old travelling song that Granny would sing when we travelled in the wagon up to Kikino for the big barn dances.

La Montagne Tortue ka-itohtanan, en charette kawitapasonan, les souliers moux kakiskenan, l'ecorce de boulot kamisahonan...

10. GOVERNMENT JOB

You want to hear a wild story? I'm sitting at my desk in a plain-ass cubicle in one of the government office towers off the legislature grounds in Edmonton. Twiddling my thumbs. Drinking Nalgene after Nalgene full of water so I have an excuse to hit up the bathroom every fifteen minutes or so. One of my friends, she always says, "When it's clear, you cheer." Well, I've been cheering since ten a.m. and it's almost four p.m. now. The lady in the cubicle next to me has been sleeping for the past two hours. I've watched as her head starts pumpjacking toward the keyboard, over and over, until she wakes with a start. Then five minutes later she's pumpjacking again.

I'm not sure if the sounds coming out of my supervisor's office are snores—if they aren't, then I don't want to know what the fuck is happening in there. But I also know that if I leave a moment before four thirty, he's going to come out all flustered and send me a passive-aggressive text about responsibilities. So I won't push my luck. It's hot outside though—like humid hot, which it never is up in the north—and I'm feeling it. I want to go swim in the legislature fountain but I'm thinking the kiddie summer camp groups won't appreciate a twenty-three-year-old bald dude yelling, "Tarps off!" and cannonballing into the two-foot-deep wading area. I'm basically sweating, sitting next to this glass window and wondering how anyone lives farther south than Edmonton. One of my friends got some crazy graduate scholarship and ended up in Montreal. That place seems next level. People die from heat there. I don't think I'll ever see her again. Montreal's out of my world.

I load up my online banking site, trying to figure out if I have enough for a few beers in case my paycheque doesn't come in right at midnight. Last few weeks, I've been in the habit of drinking heavily at this bar on the south side of the High Level on Wednesday nights, knowing that right at midnight—boom, fucking money in the bank, at least enough to cover my tab. It can get a little sketch, since they close early when they don't have enough people kicking around. I guess I'll deal with that situation when it happens. I see my balance is at $69.69 and since I'm twenty-three going on thirteen years old I start giggling and text my buddy Alex a picture.

He replies, *Fuck yeah buddy, get it.*

What you doing tonight? Beers? I message.

I'm gonna meet up with Paul later. I'll give you a shout. Thinking somewhere downtown.

Do it up. Peace.

My supervisor waddles by me, tucking his blue shirt into his brown khakis for the fifth time today and adjusting his Patagonia backpack. Buddy thinks he's an extreme hiker or something.

"Don't go to too many powwows tonight," he chirps as he walks by.

Fucking Best Buy salesman, I think to myself and flash him a gap-toothed grin. I'm fresh into this job out of the Government of Alberta's Aboriginal Internship Program, and we both know the only reason I'm here is because it's some kind of affirmative-action hire. He doesn't get the difference between Métis and Cree and just assumes every Indigenous person from Haida Gwaii to the east coast is the same. I've never even been to a powwow. Okay, I have. But he doesn't know that. The rodeo up at Kikino though, hell yeah. I'm the government's perfect candidate for affirmative action: white, bald, conversationally but not culturally fluent in Cree, bachelor's degree, enough connections to be legit, and able to hide the scary shit that they don't want to see. It's only Wednesday and I wish this week was over.

I wait until he's about five minutes gone, then I grab my fancy leather bookbag and dip out. I bought this sick rose-gold watch and bag from Southgate Centre on the first day of my internship. Man, I thought I'd made it. I was gonna make bank and help the community, work with Elders, break the fucking cycle, get off the Avenue. I was gonna be a fancy-ass downtown businessman with my watch and leather bag. A guy I know who went off the deep end in our last year of university had bought me a suit during his mental decline, so I didn't even need to hit up the thrifts. Shit, I looked good. I'm long past wearing that suit now and I left the watch at my ex-girlfriend Cheryl's place and there's no way in hell she's giving it back; guaranteed she pawned it off or threw it off the High Level Bridge. She's a poet.

It takes me about forty-five minutes to walk home. When I cross the bridge, I take a quick look down into the crystal-clear North Saskatchewan River to check if I can see that watch glimmering somewhere, even though it's probably been a year since I lost it. Just a couple tires and a skateboard down there. It's too high up for watches. My granny's brother threw himself off the bridge in his thirties but got caught up in the wires underneath and the fire department rescued him. That doesn't happen too often, especially with the new suicide prevention barriers. Granny's grandma, OG kohkom, was born right underneath the bridge, on what used to be the Papaschase First Nation territory. Granny told me that every single time we drove over it. Apparently her brother told her that when he was on the way down, he saw OG kohkom's face reflecting back at him from the river. Right when he was about to hit the water, she winked and then two eagles swooped under him and the wind gusting off their wings propelled him back up into the wires. I tell people I'm looking for that watch, but really I'd love to catch a glimpse of the original grandma. I never met her, but my dad did. The women in my family tend to live into their nineties, and my grandma told me that back before moniyaw were here, they lived well into their hundred fifties. They didn't count years back then, though. That's a new thing.

Alex gets off work around seven or eight. He works up at the Alberta Hospital doing psych aide shit with the mental patients. That's about as much as I know about it all. He's in school to be a nurse right now at MacEwan and picks up these casual shifts on the side. He still lives up on the Avenue of Champions with his aunty and uncle in an old rundown house.

They've been in that unit since I can remember. His uncle and aunty are old-school Avenue. They're local hood, and no one messes with them. Alex's about a month younger than me and I remember a night not long after we turned eighteen when we rolled into this bar off the Avenue. It was a true drinkers' bar for the locals, a place where the VLTs ran hot from open till close and the smoke poured out years after the ban went into effect. Cops only went there the morning after a shooting or a stabbing, never during. So anyways, Alex and I popped our heads into the Mona Lisa to see if his uncle and aunty would buy us a drink. His uncle ordered us two beers and two shots, Canadian Club for both, then he turned to us and said, "Alright drink up fast and get the fuck out of here." Alex and I turned around, scoped out the bar and saw a few people giving us the look you give a couple eighteen-year-olds who should know their place. "You're good for these, but after this you're on your own." His uncle continued. So we chugged and peaced the fuck out under the glint of flashing steel knives. The wrong kind of deadly shit.

I spend the rest of the walk thinking about what would happen to my supervisor if he was up on the Avenue of Champions after dark. Shit, I don't want to be up there after dark anymore and I lived there for years. We work in an area called Indigenous engagement, where we're supposed to be chatting with people in the community to hear about what's wrong. Pretty broad shit, but that's the government. I would love for an engagement session to take place at the park behind the community centre or in the bushes behind the LRT tracks. Those people would tell you exactly what the fuck is wrong. But the people there, well, they care as much about a government report as I do. In my short time working there, I've already seen a few of these "community engagement" things happen. They're always the same: white people revelling in the trauma porn of Indigenous Peoples and then writing a report after dragging up past traumas. The report sits on the shelf, and then government employees head back out the next year. Ready to rehash it all again under a different director, minister, deputy minister, whatever—it's all the same.

Don't get me wrong, I'm pretty grateful for the opportunity to have a government job. I always thought I'd be moving pallets around in some warehouse up on the north end or driving truck. Now, I'm working 7.25 hours a day for sixty K a year, more money than I thought I would ever make in a lifetime, which is alright by me. I can put up with anything for that. I mean, hell, I was homeless and living out of my car during my undergrad. After that, you can't fucking hurt me. When I told my granny that I got a government job, she was pretty choked up. I don't know what she expected from me but it wasn't that. I'm also her boy, you know, and the government hasn't necessarily always treated her and her family the best over the years. So, if her boy is now working for the Man, well shit… It was a confusing time for all of us. We had been sitting in her apartment on the north side, drinking tea, playing crib, listening to radio bingo even though she didn't have any cards, when I broke the news to her.

"Is that so?" she said.

"Yeah, it's pretty good too, you know. Make a lot of money, good hours, got, like, benefits, you know?" I tried to avoid eye contact with her, showing her the respect she deserved. In the background, you could hear the caller.

"*B* seven.

"*I* sixteen.

"*O* fifty-four.

"Wait, we got a bingo call from Shirley in Calling Lake. We're going to verify Shirley's bingo right now. Sit tight everyone, there's a big blackout game happening after this one."

A few minutes went by.

"That's a good bingo from Shirley up in Calling Lake. Okay, everyone, let's get ready for blackout."

"I guess it is what it is," Granny finally replied. Then she skunked me.

I get to my basement suite and fire up a couple jalapeno goose smokies for supper. Alex gave me tons of shit when I moved to Whyte Ave. At the time, I had been staying in the basement of one of the old white townhouses behind the Cromdale Liquor with Ashley and her mom. Cheryl and I were on a break while she went to school in Vancouver, and Ashley and I had gotten back together. Ashley's mom was the kind of lady who didn't mind that some homeless dude was shacked up with her daughter, but lost her shit if any Tupperware went missing. Her mom was heavy into pint and was always bringing by these sketchbags from the Avenue. I had been there for a few months when Ashley had finally had enough of her mom and decided that she was taking off back to Regina to go to First Nations University. No chance I was going with her to Regina, and no chance in hell I was moving back into my car. I felt this was my time to leave. Later on, I talked to Ashley about our relationship. We came to the conclusion that she basically only dated me for protection from all the shit her mom brought into their townhouse during that time. I think they figured it out though. I saw a picture of her with her mom on Instagram recently.

"Fuck, do you mean you're moving to the south side?" Alex said. We had biked over to Kingsway Mall. He wanted to steal some shoes from Sport Chek or West49. "You think you're better than us or something?"

"Nah man. I just want to get away for a bit. Try something different."

"You fucking on pint man? You don't belong over there."

"It's like a ten-minute bike ride, or you can take the train. It's not that far."

"It's a different world, man. You don't know. You get this stupid government job and now you're moving to the south side? You trying to be white? Métis people don't live on the south side."

"I'm sure some Métis live on the south side. Shit, that's where Granny said our family is from."

"Métis people don't live on the fucking south side bro. You're gonna get hammered."

"It'll be fine."

"So you do think you're better than us now?"

"No man, it's not about that. This basement suite is fucking dope, man. I don't want to live in no building we always have to leave because they're spraying it for fucking lice every two days."

"Move into the basement with me, man," Alex said.

"Dude, your room's smaller than my car. It's probably got roaches and shit too."

"Now you don't like my roaches? North side for life, you fuck."

"Fuck you, let's get your shoes and get out of here," I said.

It's been a couple years now since we had that conversation. We figured out that it wasn't that far and that even though I was on the south side, I still wasn't rich. Back when we were kids, we thought everyone who lived on the south side was rich.

I'm washing down one of the goose smokies with a Pilsner and listening to a Lucero album when my phone pings. It's a text from Alex.

Sup? Just finishing up here man. Paul and I are thinking Brewsters downtown?

Hell yeah. He can buy, I reply.

Sick. See ya in 30, Alex texts.

I check my jean jacket and a pair of green cords for mustard stains and sweat smell. They seem good to go, at least enough to pass in the darkness of a pub, and chances are I can blend out the B.O. with a solid dose of Canadian Classic smoke. The number 9 bus picks me up right outside of the basement suite. I still carry my old university ID and strategically hold my thumb over the outdated U-Pass stickers. The odd bus driver tells me to get lost, but most just don't care about it. It's not worth the confrontation for them, so I play that up. Especially since we both know it's August and even if the sticker was valid, it wouldn't kick in until September when the post-secondaries start up again.

Brewsters is bumping. We got crews from all over the city converging on a beautiful downtown summer night. I see Alex and Paul snagged a sick patio spot and are holding it down with a couple pitchers and wings already on the go. Paul's a big boy and likes the wings. He's always ordering them, even when it's not wing night. Both of them are covered neck down with tattoos and they're both wearing white muscle shirts and black jeans. If you could map out the course of Alex and Paul's lives in their tattoos, you would see that the big chest-piece owls and eagles in full colour came about when they had some cash. The shitty 780s and, in Paul's case, *fuck cops* across the knuckles in faded jail-house ink are from the bike-stealing days. They've both started to cover up the shitty ones with better, bigger, badder sleeves. But, in my opinion, nothing beats a good stick-and-poke eagle.

"Fuck boys, looking dece," I say as I walk in.

"Dan, my man," Paul says. Alex just nods at me, raises his glass and then takes a big swig.

"Paul, you hitting the gym bud? You getting mad wrecked up. Check them pipes," I say.

"Ha, what the fuck you think?" Paul says as he shoves a full hot-sauce-covered chicken wing in his mouth and then drags it out with just the bones remaining. A droplet of hot sauce falls on his white shirt and I see a group dudes on our left start laughing a bit and smirking toward Paul and our table. One of them, wearing a Lacoste polo and a backwards Oilers hat, mocks the action Paul just did, pretends to eat a wing and then moves his hands to mimic sauce splashing all over his shirt. His friends laugh. Paul's noticing the entire interaction play out, but he doesn't acknowledge it. He just winks at me and goes back to crushing wings.

"Your cousin getting out?" I ask Alex.

"Nah man, buddy put a dude's head through the wall in the cafeteria. He's got a loon on top."

"Ah shit man, I was looking forward to the party," I say.

"Shit, me too. Buddy got stacked before he went in," Alex says.

"What did he do again?" Paul asks.

"Was wasted, crashed his truck and then lit it up. Cops caught him flicking the match," Alex says.

"Only an idiot would get caught doing that," I say.

"Yeah, man, tell me about it," Alex says.

Paul finishes up his wings and I help them with their pitchers of beer. Paul gets the bill and pays straight cash.

"Alright boys, let's hit up karaoke. I could sing a tune," Alex says. I can see the group of guys who were mocking Paul earlier start laughing as he stands up. The one guy in the Lacoste polo does the same chicken-wing-eating motion. We start walking by their table. I'm in the front, Paul right behind me, then Alex. As we pass their table, I feel Paul tense up behind me. He's right behind the dude with the Lacoste polo when he turns around and clocks him right in the head with a hammer fist. The guy drops instantly. Alex has already kicked out the chair legs from under the guy beside him. The guy is walleyed on the ground and Alex boots him in the ribs and I can hear the crack. Paul smashes the knocked-out Lacoste-polo guy's head into the table one more time for good measure. Alex grabs the pitcher of beer the group had on the table and dumps it on the head of the last guy.

"Watch your place, buddy," Paul says to the guy who's now shaking, beer-drenched, while his one friend writhes on the floor and his buddy is knocked out face down at the table, blood leaking everywhere, mixing with Frank's Red Hot and chicken bones. I'm already out the door. I never stopped walking from the second Paul tensed up and it all busted out. Probably only twenty seconds have passed since Paul first hit the guy, and the other tables and bar staff are still registering what's happening. But that's enough time and we're long gone.

Paul's truck is parked around the corner, off an alley on 105th Avenue—we pile in and he starts driving toward downtown. I light up a dart and pass one up to Paul.

"You guys remember Chelsea?" Paul asks.

"Yeah, dude. Definitely," I say.

"She was rad. I wish I asked her out," Paul says.

"Dude, not too late, man," Alex says.

"Ah, she lives in Calgary now, she's big-time," Paul says.

"What, someone gets a law degree and you can't talk to them anymore?" I ask. "Sometimes I tell people I'm a lawyer."

"No one thinks you're a fucking lawyer, you clown," Alex says. He starts laughing.

"Why couldn't I be a lawyer?" I ask.

"You have a better chance of being a lawyer than Paul has of dating Chelsea. I'll give you that," he says. "Anyways, where the fuck we going boys? Night's young."

"Let's hit up Garneau? Or OJ's?" I say.

"South side… Really… Ah fuck it, why not?" Paul responds.

We pull up to a table at OJ's on 109th. The server tells us we're good to go for half-price wine night, so we order a bottle of red each.

"Please make them fancy as fuck," I say, as she takes our order.

"I don't know what that means," she responds and walks away.

We drink the first bottles and order another round. Paul has a few stories about high school and Alex talks a bit about the shit going on at the psych ward. Paul pops out for a dart a few times and I join him. Alex, somehow, has held off smoking even though everyone around him, at all occasions, is full on into it. We're back at the table and order a third round. Paul puts his head down into his phone and starts hammering away on it.

"Hey, Daniel. Remember when you used to steal books from Chapters?" Alex asks. "Fuck, you were fun then."

I laugh, "Oh man, I had that system. Open up the book and shake out that little alarm shit, then shove it in your bag." I take a drink of wine. "Shit, I must have stolen over a hundred books. Serves them right for not hiring me."

"Dude, those guys would never hire you," Alex says. "Neither would Starbucks, remember that? Those guys were shaking in the interview."

"That's because you came into the stupid Starbucks with me. Asshole," I say.

"Well, shit. I wanted a coffee."

"They saw me roll in with you. And you wouldn't shut up, so they knew I was with you," I say.

"They didn't know I was with you."

"You came and started talking to us in the middle of the interview."

"Oh man, that was fun," Alex says.

"Hey, any of you guys want to drive a van to Calgary tonight?" Paul asks.

"Fuck you," Alex and I both say.

"Man, I always feel I'm just one mistake away from being back on the Avenue," I say. The wine has hit me.

"Dude, you've never left," Alex responds.

"Okay fuck this, let's hit up downtown. South side sucks." Paul gets up, throws some bills on the table and rolls out. I look at Alex. He shrugs, stands up and follows him out.

"I'm headed home, boys," I yell at them. I finish off the wine that's left on the table and then hit the walk back to my basement suite.

It's Friday afternoon. Two days after my night out with Alex and Paul. I'm back in the office, crushing Nalgene after Nalgene, trying to get my piss clear. Trying to have more excuses to stand up and walk around. Three thirty rolls around and I get a text from Alex.

Hey man can you swing by and bring some beers and smokes?

Sure, dude. Any plans for the night? I text back.

No response.

My supervisor is making his weird noises again and I don't know if I can take another hour of it. A good cold beer sounds pretty decent, and I'd love to sit around in Alex's aunt's backyard in the sun. Maybe his sister and her friends would stop by later and we could have a real party. I decide that I'll risk the passive-aggressive text from my supervisor and besides, fuck it, I'm union and Métis. They can't do shit to me.

I head outside and get on the number 5 bus from downtown westbound up toward Ninety-Fifth Street. It's a notorious route because if you get on it heading east to Westmount and Glenora, it's filled with rich yuppies, lawyers, professionals, suits, ties, the whole works. If you get on it westbound, it's the exact opposite. Thank God it was casual day and I'm in jeans and a blue T-shirt; I wouldn't want to be that guy in a suit, that's just trouble.

There are liquor stores all over the Avenue of Champions. I head to the nearest one and grab a flat of Pilsner and a couple packs of Canadian Classics. I've got A Tribe Called Red cranked in my iPhone earbuds and I'm feeling the drum as I walk toward Alex's aunty's. When I get there, I hop the chain-link fence and head around to the backyard. I'm expecting music to be playing and Alex and probably Paul to be laying around in camp chairs, already half-cut. But it's dead. Doesn't look like anyone's been around for a while.

I open the door to the house and I can hear Alex rattling on with some story. His voice is going a thousand words a minute. I follow the voice into the dank, dark basement and an immediate mix of stale beer and urine hits my sinuses.

"Fuck are you guys doing?" I ask.

"Dan-Dan-Dan-Dan-Dan-Dan-Daniel." Alex's still scrambling around. "Did you bring the beers? Huh-huh-huh? We—just—ran—out."

"Dude, chill the fuck out." I look over at the couch. Paul is sitting there, wearing the same hot-sauce-coated white shirt from two nights ago. His eyes are wide-open beads. Alex is already into the flat of beer even though I'm still holding it. He cracks a can, slams it back and throws the empty onto the floor with countless others. I use my foot to kick empties, cigarette butts and pipes off the coffee table to make room for the flat. Alex has big black fleece blankets with wolves on them over every window. The only light is coming from the TV, which is playing YouTube videos, and a dimmed IKEA lamp in the corner. I toss Paul a beer and he catches it even though he still hasn't looked in my direction or acknowledged me. His wide-eyed stare is focused on the TV.

"You'll never guess what happened," Alex says. The beer chilled him out a bit and his words aren't flying around like they were before.

"I think I have a bit of an idea," I say.

"So after we dropped you off, man, we ended up at this bar downtown. And you know, we wanted some blow. But fucking no one's answering our calls. Anyways, Paul, he goes, 'Let's find the sweatiest dude in the room and just ask him.' So there was this guy hanging out by the bar solo, just dripping puddles. Paul goes up and asks him, 'Hey dude, you got any blow?' And then this guy, he goes, 'No, but I have a bunch of meth.' Then he says, 'If you buy me a drink, we can go smoke some.' Can you believe it?" Alex drains another beer in one long gulp, then cracks another. "So we're like, 'Fuck yeah. Let's go smoke then we'll buy you a drink.' And this guy man, he's like five six maybe, and a twig. So Paul and I, we go back into the alley behind the bar with him. He busts out this pipe and loads it up with pint. He's about to light it up, when I just look at Paul and then we start beating the fucking shit out of him. Take his backpack and his wallet. He's got about two hundy in there, and a fuck-ton of meth. So we bought two hundred dollars worth of beers and well, now here we are," Alex holds up his hands like he's some messiah of the basement mess. "We're out of the pint now, so we figure we'll ease back into it with some beers."

"You guys are fucked," I say. I sit down on the couch next to Paul, light up a cigarette and crack a beer. "Real fucked. When was the last time you slept?"

"Man, we had a fridge full of beers and a fuck-ton of meth. Why would we sleep? Okay, man, I'm going to show you this video. So many cute fucking puppies in it," Alex says.

11. BUFFALO

"You know, when I was, I don't know, ten or twelve or something, I ran away from the group home. It was another bad place, another bad place, too bad for me. And I made it pretty far and we were away for a long while. My friend came with me. I can't remember his name." Jason patted his pockets, looking for a cigarette that he knew wasn't there, but he wished so badly that it was. Across from him, a counsellor was looking across a table. He nodded at Jason to encourage him to keep talking. He looked like an older version of every social worker that Jason had ever had combined, like someone had Photoshopped all their faces together. Jason just remembered them as a blur. He remembered most things as a blur.

"I wish I could remember his name. He was a beautiful little guy. Just this tiny, tiny guy. He had a shaved head. We all had shaved heads because it was cheap and the lady running the group home could save money by doing it herself. Kinda like your haircut I guess." Jason patted his pocket again. "I really fucking wish I could smoke."

The counsellor gave Jason a look over the top of the rims of his glasses. Jason hated the way he looked at him. A mix of pity, sarcasm and a general disinterest in anything Jason had to say.

"I wonder what ever happened to that little guy," Jason said. "That day, we made it all the way across the river from the south side. We climbed through the woods in the River Valley, ran through a couple homeless camps. It wasn't cold yet. I don't remember having a jacket or a toque or anything. It must not have been cold." Jason had tried to sober up as best he could when he got into prison. He remembered coming to in the midst of withdrawal. Mosquitoes coursing through his veins, ready to explode out and continue to eat everything in their path. He remembered the mosquitoes and how they felt. How he knew what he needed to do to make them stop eating him alive. But he didn't want that anymore.

"I bet he's in prison too, or dead. We all are now. Everyone I know," Jason said. "He was so scared, too. But he didn't want to get beat anymore. I didn't either, and I hated watching him get beat. That group-home guy, I forget his name, but he was mean. Fuck, did he ever like to beat the shit out of us. I wasn't that scared though, and I saw his eyes. He was like a little brother to me, that little guy. You know, I just didn't want him to get hit. I would have taken every punch for him, every kick, it didn't matter to me. But it mattered to him. Every night I watched his eyes, and how they had faded from bright suns to dark coals."

The counsellor nodded again. Jason saw a flicker of recognition in his eyes. Something to suggest a human behind the machine. Talking felt good to Jason, it kept the mosquitoes away. Talking was a bear ready to come and breathe in all the clouds of mosquitoes. The bear would bundle them up in its stomach and run away, far away, back through time to a place where they didn't exist yet. Where they didn't torment Jason every day. The bear would sacrifice itself for Jason to make him healthy and happy. To bring him back to his aunty's table.

"Anyways, the little guy and I, we made it up the River Valley hill and then we found this beautiful concrete cave. It was right under the patio of that fancy hotel. He looked at me and asked if it could be our home. And I saw that he just wanted to be with me. We crawled into the cave, which was just this crack in the cement, just big enough for a couple kids, but too small for adults, which was probably why no one else had set up camp in it yet. Above, we could hear the voices of rich people as they ate and drank on the patio in the sun. I wondered who could be rich enough to be up there. I imagined fancy white people in big sunglasses and hats, talking about money or whatever it was that rich people talk about. What do you talk about with your rich friends?" Jason asked the counsellor.

"This is about you, Jason," The counsellor said. "Continue, please."

"Anyways, this little guy and I, we set up a really good space there. We found a couple blankets down in the River Valley that someone else had left there. I stole a whole bunch of food from the 7-Eleven, chips and pop and chocolate bars and candy. The little guy found a half-eaten pizza that someone must have chucked from a car or something. That held us over for a few days. The best part: no one could find us. I knew that if the voices from above knew there were a couple kids under them, they would call the cops. I didn't want to go back to the group home, so we stayed real hidden, real quiet-like, only really moved around at night and in the morning. We could always find where the place was because the lights on the patio and the fancy big green sign on the building above it." Jason tried to remember what they did. He just remembered laughing a lot and trying to keep the little guy entertained. If only he could remember the little guy's name. That would really help.

"I never meant to kill Charlie, you know," Jason said.

"Continue with your story, Jason. We can talk about Charlie later," the counsellor said.

"It started getting cold though. Real cold. The blankets we had and the clothes we had, they weren't enough. Then it started raining. I just remember the rain. Even though we had a great little hideout, it made the air cold and things started getting wet. There was so much rain and then thunder started. *Boom, boom, boom.* Like a gun, you know. *Boom.*" Jason moved his hand to form a pistol and he aimed it right at the counsellor. He pretended to pull the trigger and made his hand recoil back. "Ha ha you flinched, yo. You always flinch." The counsellor continued to write notes in stony silence.

"So, this little guy, he's getting scared. Like real scared. He's shivering and sitting really close to me. And I'm trying to be tough and not show him that I'm scared. You can't be scared, you know. So I started telling him a story. But it's kind of for myself too." Jason wondered if he should cry. He didn't feel like crying but it seemed to be the appropriate thing to do. Someone without mosquitoes would cry. What was the kid's name? Was it Ian? Daniel? No, Ian was a guy from the last group home they ever forced him into. Who was Daniel again?

"WHAT THE FUCK WAS HIS NAME? WHY CAN'T YOU TELL ME HIS NAME?" Jason yelled. He stood up and started pacing around the room.

"Jason, I'm going to need you to sit down."

"You have so many fucking answers to everything, why can't you tell me his name?"

"Jason, please sit down and we can continue with your story."

"I said to the kid, 'I'm going to tell you a story about a buffalo.' He looked up at me with this smile and his eyes went from coals to bright suns again. The story's kind of happy, too. It's about a big bison. This big, big, big buffalo is running around all over the prairie. He's having a hell of a time. Everywhere he looks, he's got other bison friends, and they're all having a hell of a time, too. There's good grass to eat everywhere, it grows long, the sun's always out and the rain never makes them cold, the rivers are running blue and swift and strong. The buffalo is having the best time. I would pretend to be a buffalo and I'd run around the little cave on all fours. The little guy thought that was hilarious and he started laughing real hard. I thought he was going to laugh so hard he was going to pee his pants. He might have too, I never knew because our clothes were soaked from the rain already. So this buffalo, he starts getting bored. There's not much adventure in his life. Everywhere he looks, it's just friends and food. Most of the other buffalo are content with this. They love it. They aren't craving any adventure. But this bison, well he's strong like you—is what I said to the kid—and smart, and not scared of shit. He decides that he wants to be the first buffalo to swim across the ocean. So he says his goodbyes to his family on the prairie. All the other buffalo try and warn him, 'Don't go, buffalo aren't meant to be in the ocean. We're meant for the prairie. You're going to be sorry if you go. Why would you go?' But the big buffalo is only thinking about more adventure. So off he goes, and he's running west as hard as he can. And you know how big the buffalo is? Well he jumped right over the mountains with a little hop and he landed right in the ocean. At that point in the story, I pretended to jump for the little guy and I landed in one of the puddles the rain had caused, and water splashed everywhere. Well, when that buffalo hit the water he created an earthquake and the land rippled and moved all over the world. But the buffalo didn't notice because he was in the water. He kept swimming and swimming and swimming. He started making new ocean friends, made friends with the seahorses and the turtles and the otters. They all thought the buffalo was a great swimmer. He was so big. And the buffalo found that there was lots of grass on the bottom of the ocean for him to eat. Almost as much as he'd had back on the prairie. He loved swimming so much that he kept swimming and swimming and swimming forever. Then, at one point, a turtle came up to him and said, 'Hey buffalo, you don't look like you did when you first jumped into the ocean.' The buffalo looked down at himself and instead of legs he now had fins, and instead of a big bushy coat he was smooth and sleek, and instead of horns he had big teeth and a blowhole. The buffalo had become the first whale. That's how whales were created."

"That's a good story, Jason," the counsellor said. "Thank you for sharing it with me."

"My aunty told me that one. Before she disappeared. It used to make me really happy, and it made the kid happy too. We made it through the night but the kid started getting really shaky and he started throwing up. I didn't know what to do. I got scared. I thought he might die. He could barely open his eyes, he couldn't talk to me. He was so small. I remember rubbing his back, I felt my hand was the size of his entire back. He wanted me to protect him and I couldn't. I couldn't do anything."

Jason stopped talking. His breath was getting ragged and speeding up. "FUCK I wish I had a FUCKING smoke," he yelled. Then he slumped forward in the plain brown chair and put his hands on his head. He rubbed his head, bald, where he used to have long wavy brown hair. He felt the stubble and kept rubbing it, felt each bristle and bump and hoped that his memories would just rub away.

"Do you want to continue? Or is that enough for today? We still have a bit of time," the counsellor said. "I'd encourage you to write some of these stories down. There's a program here in the prison that can help you with that."

Jason sat up and stared at him. He knew the counsellor had a hard time staring at the coal pits of his eyes. It took every bear in his body to keep the mosquitoes from spitting in the counsellor's face, jumping across the table and pummelling the fucking shit out of him. Every bear had to swallow a thousand mosquitoes. Every bear had to sprint forever with the mosquitoes buzzing around in its stomach trying to escape and get back into Jason's veins.

12. ANYTIME, ANYWHERE

It's Friday at 5:30 p.m. and the Wasenakwan Student Centre is bumping. Cree, Métis, Dene and Stoney students are scrambling to use the six desktop computers. The ones who have their own laptops are hammering away on keyboards from anywhere that they can find a place to sit. The staff in the centre are running back and forth from student to printer to photocopier. It's scholarship deadline day and the mad scramble is on to get applications in. For most of the students, scholarships can make or break their ability to attend the community college next semester. If they don't get anything, they're out, forced to take a semester off. Then next year they'll try all over again, complete the endless applications for band or Métis funding, government funding, individual scholarships and awards.

I don't get too involved with scholarship deadline day. My input is irrelevant at this point. I'm outdated, and the words I used to write for scholarships don't get anyone anything anymore. When I was a student and for the few years afterwards, it was all about writing to bring the fire. Writing in the applications why the hell systems were failing Indigenous Peoples. Bring as much heat as possible and try to make the person reading the application sweat or cry tears of reconciliation. No one wants to hear that now. They just want to hear about how you're going to use the funds to get a degree and then get a job in the oil field. If it isn't oil-field-based, then it won't go through, unless maybe you're talking about being a dutiful housewife to a good old oil-field-working boy and supporting him with a part-time administration gig that this diploma will enable you to get.

There was that glory moment. Well, I don't know if *glory* is the right word to use. It happened right after the Truth and Reconciliation Commission's final report rolled through Canada. The country opened up for First Peoples in a way it hadn't before. Universities, colleges, governments, corporations— everyone started hiring Indigenous people into positions of perceived authority and privilege. I rode the fuck out of that wave. My friends and I hit it perfectly when we came out of our undergraduate and graduate degrees in the mid-2010s. We all got jobs nearing six figures and were invited to tables and boardrooms that historically we had been shut out from. And we hit those meetings and our positions with the intensity we had from our peoples' grassroots and community-organizing days. At each one, we started switching narratives, changing policies and procedures, the whole works. We met with senior leadership, told people to smarten the fuck up. We kept saying that Indigenous voices and lives mattered across this country. For a hot minute, we thought people were listening and that we had finally created a wave big enough that it would be unstoppable. A new reality and story for First Peoples in this country.

Then it ended. The Wet'suwet'en crisis was the tipping point. Indigenous Peoples started rising up on a scale that settler Canadians paid attention to. The government realized that they didn't want to deal with that. Reconciliation was great when everyone got to wear a headdress and parade around with cute brown kids and learn about smudging. When it came time for equity though, fuck that. Canadian society spoke up when the protests started and they basically said that they wanted to forget Indigenous Peoples existed. The media turned on us; though they were never really on our side to begin with. The racists got louder. Even the so-called allies decided we were an inconvenience.

We realized at that point that we had never actually made any progress. Everything was just for show. That our ten years of pushing forward amounted to shit all. Elders had told us along the way that it was just a cycle and that this had happened before for brief moments in the seventies and nineties. Our youthful arrogance made us think that this time would be different. But it wasn't, and we got smoked. Our jobs remained, for the most part. My friends who got professor gigs got to keep them. But the Indigenous studies and Native studies department budgets got slashed to fuck. The institutions were just waiting for the proper moment to dissolve the departments altogether. Ministries like Indigenous Relations were long gone. They were the first to go under the pretense that every good public servant should be doing Indigenous relations. But they weren't, and they never did. A line like that is how you sell bullshit to the public though.

I'm one of those people who has managed to hold on to my job. I'm forty-three, I've been the manager of Waskenakwan

Student Centre for fifteen years now. I'm outdated, like I mentioned, in more ways that one, and I really shouldn't be here anymore. I should have left when I turned thirty-five, but it's a good paycheque, and I'll be able to retire with a full pension when I'm fifty-five. Can you get more colonized than that? I'm sure I'll get fired before then. But honestly, I really don't want to go back to the way I lived during my undergraduate degree and the years before then. People glorify that inner-city existence, but it fucking sucked. I did not have a good time. I'm comfortable now. I live on the south side. I have a little house. I don't have methed-out cousins and friends showing up at my place anymore. They're all long gone. The house has a garden. It's more than I ever thought I'd have. I'm too soft now to go back. Too much belly fat and not enough hair.

I don't pretend that we're changing anything. I don't have illusions that our work is going to make a difference. Honestly, I should have known better at the start. But I was still under the impression that this was it. That all these stupid little Indigenous awareness sessions were going to be the change in Canada. I'd pour my heart out setting up professional development sessions for non-Indigenous professors and instructors who claimed that reconciliation was all that mattered. That if there were more PD sessions offered, they would attend all of them. So I'd call in favours and search for amazing young speakers. They brought up new topics and cutting-edge research and created new voices in Indigenous education. I'd raise money of my own accord to pay them honorariums, or put myself out of pocket. We'd set up these sessions during work hours so people could attend. Our hearts and souls would be drained in the creation of these opportunities for non-Indigenous staff. Because we wanted them to learn new ways of thinking and being, and start on the journey of reconciliation with us. Because we believed in it and our work. And after all of that, we'd have four people show up, and two of them were staff from the Wasenakwan Indigenous Student Centre.

The staff would give all the excuses. Say they'd be there at the next one. But they never were. And eventually we just stopped putting these sessions on. Because why bother? Why care when no one else did? Society shifted, the conversation stopped and eventually people even stopped making those claims around supporting reconciliation. And I could give a shit. I used to give a shit. By the time it ended, fuck it.

I'm not really sure how I ended up in this world. It's all a blur. It seems like yesterday that I was a kid watching my older brother Charlie playing hockey at the McCauley–Boyle Street outdoor game. He was a damn good player, could have had a bit of a career if he had been given the opportunity. But opportunities didn't exist for us then. They definitely don't exist now. Not for Charlie. He's been dead for, shit, almost twenty years now. A guy we grew up with stabbed him in the midst of a meth bender. It's tough for me to remember Charlie as an actual person. He's been gone for so long.

I'd be lying if I said I wasn't lonely. If it weren't for the Labrador retrievers that are kicking around, I would have shot myself years ago. But the dogs are beautiful and every minute that I get to spend with them gets me through the days. I used to visit Granny. She's long gone now too. Granny died when she was ninety-three. Just like she always told me she would. All the women in our family call it at ninety-three. And sure enough, she was sitting there playing crib with her buds a couple weeks after her ninety-third birthday and she just up and croaked, with a glass of her crabapple bounce on the table beside her. Pretty poetic if you ask me.

She never approved of my career. Thought it was a waste of my efforts and passion and that I would've been better off doing something that didn't involve selling out to the government and education systems. I disagreed with her back then. But that was when I still thought that we had hit our "TSN turning point" in creating equity for Indigenous Peoples. But now it makes sense. Granny was right. Even when I was winning all these white awards and getting a lot of publicity for my cultural programming work, she always disapproved. Although I once got twenty-nine when we were playing crib and she talked about that for ten years straight.

I'm fat now. Too many beers and hot dogs. I did everything that I was supposed to do. Degree, check. Government internship, check. Career, check. Only thing I missed was the getting married and settling down part. No kids, which is fine by me. This world's already hard enough for those who are here. Though I do miss the days when I volunteered for Big Brothers Big Sisters. That was fun, going to the pool and hitting up the diving boards and slides with the kids. Shit, that was almost twenty years ago now too. I did that kind of thing right when I first started working. When I had all the energy in the world to bound around and share the fortune of my intern salary. I thought I was so cool at the time because I was making bank and worked downtown. No meth benders on the north side for me. I just ended up living vicariously through my buddy Alex.

Alex's gone too. Not dead. But he ended up meeting a doctor at a tattoo convention and peacing out to Vancouver where she works. He's doing dad life now with a couple kids. He picks up the odd nursing shift here and there, but mainly stays at home with the kids while Vanessa—I think that's her name—works crazy emergency-room doctor hours. She's a straight gangster. That's a tough life. Tougher than anything I've ever had to do.

I used to date this one lady, Cheryl. She tuned me up. We were on and off for a bit while she went to Vancouver for social work school. Mainly off when she was there and on when she was back in the city. She was the one who got me out of the Avenue of Champions life and into thinking about creating new narratives for Indigenous Peoples. After she became a social worker, she started advocating for young First Nations women who were being thrown around by the systems that were meant to protect them. She wore her heart on her sleeve and was always cruising around finding women and giving them all her love and support. She'd always be bringing whole van loads of women out to the First Nations to meet up with Elders and go to ceremony. I'd tag along to drive the van so Cheryl could chat with the young women. I learned a lot from her family about ceremony and protocol. Teachings I wouldn't change for the world. All that experience was better than anything I ever learned in university. Lots of those old Elders helped me out even after Cheryl and I split.

We broke up after Charlie went down. I couldn't deal and I took it out on Cheryl. Not any violent shit or anything like that.

Just straight shutting down emotionally. I was never a big feelings guy to begin with and after that, fuck man, I don't know. Just something in me left with Charlie and I've never been able to get it back. Cheryl left not long after, too. I still see her around at community events. She's got a bunch of cute-ass kids and a moose-hunting husband who seems like a legit dude. No problem there.

I really don't know why I'm writing all this down. Something about trying to process my emotions. Former girlfriends always said I needed to get better at sharing feelings and shit like that. But it's been hard, and man, after Charlie got shanked up I shut down a lot. That guy meant the world to me. I hope Jason gets the fuck beat out of him on the daily down in Stony Mountain or wherever he ended up. I'm never forgiving that fuck. Even though at one point he wrote me a letter talking about it and about how he did wrong.

I haven't told many people this, but I think I'm the real reason Charlie got killed. Jason's always been fucked up. If you take one look at the guy, you know he's not all there. I'm sure he's been diagnosed with absolutely everything from FASD straight to ADHD and everything in between. And the drugs never helped him. Though I couldn't fully blame him, with where he came from and the group homes that he was always in. He never left with Granny. He had to ride it out. Really though, it comes down to the fact that I shouldn't have told Jason that Charlie had hit it big at the casino. That was basically the same as putting out a hit on someone. I forgot my place, and where I was, and who I was talking to. I was just excited that Charlie had some cash for the first time in his life. But that one line ended it all. Fuck Jason and fuck his stupid little AA letter or whatever that bullshit was. If I ever run into him again, I'm going to put a bullet in each of his kneecaps and then one in the back of his skull.

13. GRANNY

"I hear you, my boy."

I see my grandmother's face in every notokesiw that sits outside the stores that run up and down the Avenue of Champions. I hear her laugh in every ask for spare change from the moniyaw walking past. I see her bones and blood in every blade of grass, every leaf and needle, every speck of dirt, every drop of rain. Her voice is in the mufflers of the motorcycles and the laughter of the drunk university students. Her footsteps shuffle back and forth across the land where her ancestors were born. Past the concrete boxes of bars, restaurants, pawn shops, liquor stores, clothing stores, cheap trinket stores and vintage stores.

When I walk this avenue, underneath the boarded-up Burger Baron's, coffee shops and money loan marts, I think of her carrying me along as a child. I think of her showing me home. Buildings come down. Buildings go up. It's hard to remember that she moved to the Island when everything in this city carries her story.

She used to get her news from eavesdropping on the conversations of smokers and people drinking beer on patios. She had become invisible to their eyes, and they stared right through her. What she didn't understand from their words, she filled in with her imagination. To her there was no difference in the importance of national politics and teen girl drama. We used to sit on the bench outside the karaoke lounge chain-smoking borrowed cigarettes and talking.

"Did you hear that Andrew and Megan hooked up last night and she forgot her boyfriend's hoodie in Andrew's room?"

"namoya Granny. Not that one."

"What about Trudeau being into men?"

"What?"

"Pfft. You're out of it, my boy."

When her sisters were young, they would get her to buy the booze. "You're the white one," they'd chant in unison. "You don't get in any trouble." So she'd put on her reddest lipstick, a fake wedding ring and her nicest dress to wander over to the liquor store and pick up some cheap wine. Her mother often said to her, "You're lucky. You can pass. Your sisters, now, they're in trouble."

I see her in the ladies I work with at the Friendship Centre. They need the drink to stop the shake. They shake so bad they can no longer place the tiny red, blue and white beads on their needles without it. The door of the drop-in centre says, *No booze, drugs or weapons*, but these ladies need a nip to be able to bead. And the old man who runs the program doesn't care. That sign is for the young people, or the ones who scream in tongues, not the old ladies from the Avenue.

In the summers, I see her sleeping behind the old brick public library building or under the Mill Creek Bridge. She had this big old blanket, red faded to orange, with a bison skull on it. The blanket never left her side. She called me from Vancouver Island years ago and told me that when she died, I should throw her in the river because she wanted to see her cousin who'd moved to Prince Albert one last time. The other day, I sat on that same bench I used to sit on with Granny when a young woman shuffled by me with the blanket on her shoulders. I thought I heard her whisper, "I hear you, my boy."

ACKNOWLEDGEMENTS

For all the Indigenous kids out there who were or are currently being taken from loving families just because you dared to exist. For all the Indigenous kids out there who weren't or aren't able to make it home. You deserve better than what this failed colonial experiment of a country gave you. Know that you're loved. Always were. Always will be.

Fuck you to all the teachers, cops, social workers, professors, administrators, politicians and bureaucrats that enacted and carried out inconceivable genocidal policies against Indigenous Peoples and continue to do so.

The land doesn't forget and neither do we.

Ten years. I guess that's a long time. Jesse, Alex, Jasmine, Ricky, Ashley, we may all have went our own ways, but I love all of you and will carry you in my story forever. I hope you see the best of yourselves in these.

All the love for MacEwan University's kihew waciston and NorQuest College's Indigenous Student Centre and the incredible students and staff in these spaces. I feel very fortunate to have spent so much time learning, laughing, and starting an Insta-famous beadwork and baloney company with you all.

I've been very fortunate to have been supported by so many friends and family over the years including but not limited to: Kristen Miller, Doug Lemermeyer, Marie Bird, Jackie Rain, Tibetha Kemble, Elliott Young, Terri Suntjens, Kelsey Reed, Amber Dion, Jonathan Robb, Jeremy Albert, George Desjarlais, Adam Ambrozy, Taylor Rubin, Leaha Atcheynum, Kerrie Gladue, Melissa Purcell, Rocky Morin, Delores Cardinal, Bob Cardinal, Joe Ground, Wilson and Charlene Bearhead, Jamie Medicine Crane, the late Metis Elders Alvena Strasbourg and Gloria Laird. You all do so much to support communities and our youth. I'm constantly inspired by your dedication. I'll pay you all back in moose and ducks someday.

My brothers Sam, Aaron and Ryan. Maybe not Ryan. Scratch Ryan's name from this.

Big shoutout to the UBC MFA program, especially Erin Steele, Jaclyn Adomeit, Manj Sidhu, Trina Moyles and everyone else who workshopped the stories in this novel into publications. Kalie for the initial edits. And of course my supervisor Maureen Medved for helping me get that Aboriginal Graduate Fellowship despite my solid 2.1 undergraduate GPA.

The following literary magazines and anthologies for giving space to my fiction writing:

An earlier version of "The Bake Sale" was shortlisted for *The Malahat Review*'s Novella Prize in 2020. A shorter, edited version received an honourable mention in *Prairie Fire*'s 2020

Short Fiction Contest. This version was published in the 2021 summer issue of *Prairie Fire*.

"Skating Circles" was first published in the spring 2021 issue of *Prairie Fire*.

"Prairie" was first published in the winter 2020 issue of *This Magazine*.

"Bridges" was first published in the fall 2020 issue of *The Fiddlehead*.

"The Last Big Dance" was first published in the winter 2019 issue of *The Malahat Review*. It was anthologized in *Best Canadian Stories 2020* (Biblioasis).

"Granny" was first published in *Write Across Canada: An Anthology of Emerging Writers* (Book*hug Press, 2019).

PHOTO CREDIT: Zachary Ayotte

ABOUT THE AUTHOR

Conor Kerr is a Métis/Ukrainian educator, writer and harvester. He is a member of the Métis Nation of Alberta, part of the Edmonton Indigenous community and is descended from the Lac Ste. Anne and Fort des Prairies Métis communities and the Papaschase Cree Nation. His Ukrainian family settled in Treaty Four territory in Saskatchewan. Conor works as the manager of Indigenous relations and supports at NorQuest College and is a sessional instructor in the pimâcihisowin program at MacEwan University. In 2019, Conor received *The Fiddlehead*'s Ralph Gustafson Poetry Prize. His writing has been anthologized in *Best Canadian Stories 2020*, *Best Canadian Poetry 2020* and has appeared in literary magazines across Canada. He is honoured to be able to live, work and chase Labrador retrievers around on the land that his family has called home for generations.